Maybelleen

ALSO BY KATHLEEN WALLACE KING

The True Life Story of Isobel Roundtree

Maybelleen

A Novel

Kathleen Wallace King

Henry Holt and Company
New York

Henry Holt and Company, Inc.
Publishers since 1866
115 West 18th Street
New York, New York 10011

Henry Holt ® is a registered
trademark of Henry Holt and Company, Inc.

Published in Canada by Fitzhenry & Whiteside Ltd.,
195 Allstate Parkway, Markham, Ontario L3R 4T8.

Library of Congress Cataloging-in-Publication Data
King, Kathleen Wallace.
Maybelleen: a novel/Kathleen Wallace King.—1st ed.
          p.   cm.
            I. Title.
PS3561.I4798M38   1995   94-31879
813'.54—dc20   CIP

ISBN 0-8050-3600-8

Henry Holt books are available for special promotions
and premiums. For details contact: Director, Special Markets.

First Edition—1995

DESIGNED BY BETTY LEW

Printed in the United States of America
All first editions are printed on acid-free paper.∞

1   3   5   7   9   10   8   6   4   2

This book is for my ancestors
and, as always, for Kurt.

My thanks to Richard Erdoes and Alfonso Ortiz for recording the Cheyenne story of creation in their book *American Indian Myths and Legends*.

I want to go out in the smoke and die with my boots on.
—Bill Tilghman, Marshal,
Dodge City, Kansas

Maybelleen

Margaret
1960

What if you were in the deepest woods; no, more than that. A forest. Trees so thick they blinded the sky. No. Even more. It is night and the trees are still so thick about you that you feel you might suffocate. You walk with arms outstretched. You can see nothing. You collide with tree after tree after tree and inside you begin to feel a scream building. But you keep it in. The minute it escapes you know that you have released the thing inside you that you can't hope to contain.

This is how I try to write it—how I felt before I know what I know now. There really are no words to describe walking on the edge of the deterioration of the self. But I found myself; or I found what I believe to be me through

Maybelleen. I don't know if Maybelleen truly ever found what she needed, but I believe that she did. It's very important to me to believe that.

We all walk around in a nighttime forest. At least sometimes. I found my way out.

This is how.

North Texas
1902
Mexican Bill and Maybelleen

She was wrapped up in smoke and dreams and clouds. Smoke rising from the tiny mesquite campfire. Dreams of feeling old as earth. She coughed because she'd caught cold. She laughed because she'd still cough when he was dead.

Up above pale clouds flirted round the man in the moon. Drifting about on the lake of her mind her thoughts whirl-pooled, searching for shore while Mexican Bill lay dying in her lap.

Scraps of things kept floating by. And popping up, long submerged, these memories rose to the surface and rocked about. The dining room table back in Kentucky with its bees-wax shine gleamed in her mind like a holy relic. "May, honey, I don't know what I'd do without you," said Ivy over and over. "Mama's little baby likes shortnin', shortnin', Mama's little baby likes shortnin' bread." She heard hands clap in a rhythm she couldn't quite make out; like patty-cake, but no, more like drums and more like aaa ya ya ma, aaa ya ya ma.

The blood had stopped but his breath came hard. She knew he was dead with the sun. He'd closed his eyes and shut up his soul.

"We'll hit 'em like lightnin'."

And when he died before the next day of her life, died right there as close as can be, he'd still be warm.

Above her a million stars were white and flickering. "Like ice" out loud, she said. She raised her head and watched the turning of them and then she buried him down into the sandy ground she sat upon.

She heard the final thud of his body, rolled into the shallow grave they'd hurriedly dig—because they were running and couldn't do it right—smelled the absolute dryness of the earth that would cover him.

There were handfuls of dirt hitting his body. Dry dirt raining down on his body. She listened to the hissing of countless tumbling pebbles. She watched them cover his dark pocked face. She saw him wrapped up forever. Those beautiful lips that had sung to her and had covered up her own now spoke with earth, not with her. Not ever again would they sing to her.

Up above the stars whirled on.

She sat and watched it all before it happened. She above-ground and him below.

But he breathed on.

Ragged, sharp, were those sighs he made. As though each breath was a stabbing knife. She smoothed his hair, ran that long black hair through her fingers, untwisting every knot.

She wouldn't kiss him a last time, would not kiss him good-bye. "You saved me, Bill," she said. She'd always say that.

But he was still dying.

And then she felt herself all hot inside. This is rage she thought. That's the word, this is what it means.

There was no glory. There was no reason.

Shot like a rat in a corncrib. For what? All his arguments, all his talk of this here and that there had got him was a hole in the ground. Robbing a bank was robbing a bank. That's what it came down to. His someday Indian nation was a phantom and had never heard of Robin Hood anyway.

Something inside her lifted up. It sniffed. Her eyes burned hot enough to melt the rocks that ringed all around them. Her teeth tasted metal. She felt a scream coming up mixed with all her insides that would surely drive death away.

But she kept it in, that scream, and the rage gradually grew cooler, until it was as blue-cold as the stars above.

The moon sailed on and on above in its nest of a thousand worlds. And for just that moment, she felt almost nothing.

She sat in the desert and watched as the heavens above slowly danced her fortune.

He stirred for a moment. His breath sputtered. Aaaah she readied inside herself. But then he settled again and breathed the same.

Then a coyote yipped, sharp and high, not too far away. And another and another until their cries wrapped her in a circle.

She thought then, as that moon peeked from behind those veiling clouds, how true love was a winding sheet to be placed forever with the dead. How love was a carrier of corpses for ten thousands of years. How love left blind hands behind pat-patting on walls, looking for a door through which grief might crawl. And someone left behind with nothing but the winding sheet.

Her heart went beat and beat and wouldn't stop no matter if she held her breath. She coughed.

"I believe you, Bill," she said to herself or to him or to the stars.

She'd never understand why no one else ever did. Was a good thing that hard to believe?

Not even they'd believed him. These men. But they liked him. They even loved him. Bill had a magic that their hearts had grabbed. Only that. Nothing else. Because that kind of feeling doesn't come with reason. And Bill was far from reasonable.

Funny how her eyes saw different now. Different things a different way. She saw far back to the farm in Kentucky and lilacs growing down below her safe, lace-framed window. She saw the farm in cold greens and blues rolling on to an empty horizon. And she realized that nothing was ever as it appeared to be. People always got it wrong. They twisted things and worried them until they got things the way they wanted.

That was history.

Bill never moved again in her lap. She bent her head down and twisted her ear to his mouth. He breathed still.

Almost dead, she saw that he was just about ugly. Deep-pitted skin and eyebrows that grew together on a low, creased forehead. Alive he'd been the handsomest man she'd ever imagined.

Then also, there was a poem she was trying hard to remember.

They'd never really believed him. Those two.

Big Shoe nodded beside the dying fire, each line on his face drawing a map to somewhere. Good true Shoe. "Hey crip, hey hog foot," people would call when he walked by. What did he believe?

Well, he'd tried to stay awake with her but he just couldn't. He'd taken a bullet in the forearm but had kept on riding behind her, backing her up, firing from the rear where the guns could get him first. Shielding her.

You had to believe something to do that.

Now he was a dead man too.

And so was the time. So was the time. She knew it, she knew too much and wished she'd never known anything at all.

Was it ever any different? Was there ever any other time? Maybe it had always been the same and there's never been anything but legends, only stories. No Jason, no Ulysses. No hanging gardens, no hill of skulls.

And he hadn't been a hero to anyone but her.

Because he'd believed. That was just about the biggest miracle she'd ever seen. Only thing close to a miracle, really.

What was that poem? She'd always been good with poems.

Beside Shoe, his head on his silver-worked Mexican saddle—how proud he was of that lovely saddle—Black Vitus snored. His snorts were just as rhythmic and reasoned as he was himself.

Here's a man with no dark dreams, she thought. There was nothing twisting in the dreams of Vitus to sort out, or fly above. No falling into the mind's deep caverns. If Vitus dreamed at all, it was of tiny, dancing angels, pirouetting and kicking like dance-hall girls. He didn't dream up legends. He only believed in here and now. And he certainly wasn't dreaming Bill's death. They just couldn't figure Bill dying.

Well, if they could sleep while Bill was dying that showed a certain confidence in things. Even with all those holes in him he hadn't died yet.

Now the fire was just a dim red glow, a few cracklings as a branch died. Tiny sparks flew up and made their own little universes. She heard the coyotes sniffing round about them, looking for scraps and sniffing the wind.

Only Young Pup stayed awake—still watched her across the fire with those gray eyes. Only Pup knew Bill was almost gone and he couldn't help himself. He was trying to tell her he was there, ready to step in.

And another time she might have let herself understand, having been on the other end herself. But she kept hearing that song in her head. Put it in the oven and bake it, bake it . . . the song got in the way of that poem she couldn't remember.

Please see me, please see me, please love me May.

The boy's eyes had never left her through the night. Across the dying fire he'd stared his love at her.

But her love was weaving a winding sheet for Bill. The birds began to sing. Birds will sing in the desert, birds will sing. She'd been surprised to hear them, when she'd first ridden away with Bill, singing out in the strangest places.

She listened now and heard them better with the dying of her heart. Now she had a ghost heart.

"My ghost heart," she said aloud, and Pup tilted his head, as though he understood.

When finally after a thousand years the sun came up, she looked directly at it so that it would burn out her eyes. But she couldn't keep them open long enough.

So she kept her vision and Bill died.

He just died. No last stirring, no final deep sigh, no calling out to her. In fact, she wasn't sure exactly when he did die. Could have been while she'd stared into the sun or an hour before while that song twisted around in her head and the coyotes yipped.

But he was certainly dead.

She realized she'd always known he would be from the moment that they'd met. And that she was going to hang when they caught her.

What would that be like she wondered, as she sat there on a cold North Texas prairie, far away from blue Kentucky, with her dead man in her lap.

She sat there and sat there, until they finally had to pry him away, her dead man, and put him in that shallow grave.

"What now, May?" they asked her then. They had no one else to ask.

"What now?"

She looked up at them and said,

> " 'A traveler, by the faithful hound,
> Half-buried in the snow was found,

Still grasping in his hand of ice
That banner with the strange device,
Excelsior!

"There in the twilight cold and gray,
Lifeless, but beautiful, he lay,
And from the sky, serene and far,
A voice fell, like a falling star—
Excelsior!' "

The men hung their heads. They thought it was a prayer.

"There, I remembered." She had the strongest desire to get down on her hands and knees and swallow the dirt around Bill's grave. But of course she didn't.

"Well," said one, putting on his hat again. And Young Pup squinted at the horizon like he expected someone or something to come.

"We ride the money down to Mexico, boys. Like he wanted," she said.

Black Vitus laid something on top of the grave.

"What's that?" said Shoe.

But Vitus didn't answer. Maybelleen turned and saw it was a rusty nail.

"Them Indians ain't never comin', May," Shoe said.

"Doesn't matter. There's talking and there's doing. You know what he said."

From behind, her ghost ears caught Shoe as he said, "What you put that nail on his grave for?"

She saddled her horse.

"To keep off the devils," Vitus replied.

She swung up on the mare and turned it away from the night and her dead man.

Margaret
1958
Jefferson County, Kentucky

DAY ONE

Sometimes you get to a place in life where it all falls to pieces. One day everything made sense. The future was that faraway time when you would finally be happy. That, I think, is what you would call hope.

Then things happen. One thing happens to set you back, set you reeling, and then along comes another thing until you stagger under the weight of that accumulated pile of events.

Or maybe nothing happens.

When the doctor told my husband that I was suffering

from nerves, that I had had a breakdown, I watched his face.

What a funny place the world is. How falsely we secure our lives. When Jack heard it put into words, it all changed overnight. I guess to Jack it meant I was now different, somehow deficient. Something broken. Something he was incapable of fixing. And that made him angry. At me. I betrayed him like a good car in which the engine goes.

Maybe marriage isn't much different than playing house when we're children because we usually marry under the same illusions. I think that perhaps those childhood fantasies are even stronger. We truly believed them. With faith. Total and unequivocable rock-solid faith.

But I have to say that his face broke my heart.

Jack wouldn't look me in the eyes in the doctor's office, and afterward when he did, it was never in the same way. His new face was full of doubt and a hundred fears. Suddenly I saw that the man I married was afraid. Afraid of everything.

And I saw him struggle. I watched him try, but it didn't work. Every time he looked at me after that one night, that night when I just couldn't think of an honest reason to keep going, I could see what he was thinking: Will she really lose it now, will she go over the edge?

And, how will I cope? What will I do?

And from then on we lived in the world of I. I with me

and Jack with himself. We never touched again except by accident and never again would there be we. I saw him afraid and he saw me. Afraid.

And I realized we always had been.

So he hid all the knives in the kitchen and had the gas range replaced with an electric. If I hadn't been down in such a hole I would've seen how funny that was. As though I could ask a kitchen appliance to lend a hand. As though I could sit on cold linoleum with my head stuck in the oven like too-big poultry.

If we had an argument and I went to look out the window I could see him thinking how high up our apartment was and the futility of even trying. And of course he was right, he couldn't think of everything. And in fairness I guess that would weigh anyone down.

Now, far away from that face I can be less selfish. Less self-involved. It can't be too comforting to hear that your wife is off-balance and maybe always will be.

"Is there any history of . . .?" That must have kept ringing in his head. Because he didn't know and neither did I.

Heredity.

So then he drank more. My Jacky. And I can't say that I didn't help him along. I drank too. We would drink and then we could have a laugh or two. Or, he could smack me. Either way, drunk, we could still play house. We could pretend to be we.

But I just couldn't ever get drunk enough. I couldn't ever drink the oceans of alcohol it would take to kill the grayness spreading inside.

Finally he left.

I turn this over and over in my mind. All the promises of love beyond the grave, of love that would never die, and yet, all it took to rip that up was one night of complete despair.

A fairy tale. Love.

Seventeen days I laid in bed. Sixteen nights after he was gone.

Then I remembered Maybelleen.

She floated up through the dead lead in me like an invading, new-created atom and burst wide-open into consciousness. All this time I'd been remembering something. Then it clicked.

Maybelleen.

Gone crazy and got hanged.

Finally the link.

I got out of bed, got dressed, and drove the Chevy through day and night. I don't remember ever stopping.

First thing when I got to the farm I took off all my clothes. I used to do that when I was a little girl. I'd take off my clothes in the summer sun and run around naked. There was no one to see me—people were miles away. I'm not sure what I was thinking but it had something to do with getting in contact.

My thirty-five-year-old body is a different place than my nine-year-old body was, yet when I took off my clothes everything came back to me. I remembered how clean is summer air.

Lying in the overgrown pasture this afternoon I was surrounded by clover and bees and the smell of ripe grass. I watched the bees about their business. How fat and serious they are in clover.

I could lie surrounded by bees and never be stung. I was nothing more than a log or a heap of leaves to them. They go about their business in a straight line. And I wished that I could too. But my straight lines have tiny curves and exits here and there so I never seem to get anywhere at all.

But then I lifted myself from my bee bed and walked up to the little cemetery above the lake.

I saw a dragonfly. Its wings were thirty colors and I couldn't tell you one of them. There were dried cow pats underfoot, petrified by sun and ice. This farm has become an ancient site, I think, as I walk through the goldenrod and dandylions. A place for excavation. There's nothing here anymore but fossils and memories.

And just me looking to dig things up.

From the road the graveyard is about a quarter mile through pasture. My bare feet chased away grasshoppers and I found a ladybug crawling up a milkweed stalk. How high, I thought, that ivory pod must seem to her, and how secure, as she swayed a thousand insect feet above the dark ground.

Ladybug, ladybug fly away home, your house is on fire and your children alone. I stubbed my toe more than once on something old and rusting away in the field.

I don't have summer feet anymore. I found myself thinking I'd build them up like I used to do when I was little by walking on the gravel in the road. Build up the calluses till my soles were like leather. As if I'll be here that long.

Behind me as I walked was the hole in the ground where the house used to stand. The house is gone now. It exploded.

Isn't that a funny thing? A house exploding. It's not what you'd think would happen to a house.

The house blew up when the furnace overheated one freezing night ten years ago. And when the house blew up my grandparents blew up too. Nothing was left but a hole in the ground and all this Kentucky earth surrounding it.

It's all mine now. This place I never wanted and went so far away from. I look back at the horizon where the white house used to sit and it comes and goes in front of me. I can make it as real as I want for just a second.

But it's really not there at all.

Yet, walking forward everything looks the same as it did when I was little. Walking forward the trees still ring the lake and the graveyard still stands there above it, littered with fallen marble from the markers.

I'm lifted up. The air is like silk, the way it smooths over me. I sing, I come naked to them here.

I walked among the graves, touching them, feeling the roughness of the granite, the smoothness of the marble. A singular cold, white angel still stands in the center with hands clasped. That pure white angel's still praying someone to heaven. But what I was looking for wasn't the angel or even the shiny new granite of my grandparents' graves.

Mama's little baby likes shortnin', shortnin'. I pick up acorn caps as I go along. I'll make a necklace and wear it to bed. I feel the blood in me and I smell things growing underground.

Then I find it. The other one. A limestone block in pale green and veined with yellow far off to the side, at the furthest edge. I brush away the leaves and wipe away the dirt.

This marker is laid into the ground. It doesn't rise up to heaven or have a finger pointing to the sky. It doesn't read GONE HOME. It just says MAYBELLEEN MACGREGOR, 1902.

They got her body back in 1918.

I stood there for a long time, looking down at the piece of rock and I felt the same way I'd felt those long years gone when I'd done the same thing, standing there in my lonely skin. A creeping feeling went through me from the soles of my feet, up through my legs, through the center of my being to the back of my head.

I was standing on her.

I was standing on her and I could feel her down there

below me, twisting and turning. She's never rested easy, this great-aunt of mine. But her blood is what binds me. She's all I'll ever know. Mother, sister. Maybelleen.

And the thousand tears that I could never cry since Jack left me, since the grayness got me, fell out of my eyes and over the ledge of my chin and went rolling down to Maybelleen until finally I threw myself upon her in the hot summer grass, displacing all the little things that lived there and still I cried and cried.

Finally I pulled myself up and sat, the dry grass indenting my skin, holding my knees close into me, my tears falling between my legs.

"Maybelleen," I said, "I'm so lost, so lost. I'm wandering without touching anything and I don't know what to do."

Of course she heard me. She always has.

DAY TWO

I'm sitting here singing "Go Down Moses" but getting to the promised land is becoming harder and harder.

I'm sitting on top of the well, the cistern cover is pebbly concrete and hurts. I'm sitting on top of the well singing just the same as when I was little.

Sitting here, the same old elm tree throws shadows on the high grass around me. Branches wave above and move the shadows around and around.

"Hey, good old tree," I say. "I used to hug you."

I used to believe that trees have souls. When I found a tree that had been cut down I used to cry. A cut tree always looked so hurt to me. But when I was small I believed so many things. Maybe all those things are still true and just seem different to me now. If that's so, if they are the same, why is it I can't feel them the same?

I see the honeysuckle growing insanely around the fence posts in the supper garden. That smell makes me think of summer-brown bodies and rhubarb pie. In this way, I'm home. If I don't look at the ripped ground behind me, I could almost believe that hardly anything has changed.

And down below me in the well the whales swim on serenely, absorbing my disturbance above. They're down there still providing their oracular strength. Whales in a Kentucky well or a sibyl at Delphi are just the same. They are. Faith is the ticket on the train to redemption.

I pull up some grass and chew the white roots. Remembering. How the days then were full of high clouded skies and you never noticed a day had gone away forever.

In those days, I convinced Malcolm that there were whales swimming around in the well. My brother believed almost anything I told him then.

"What whale?" he'd asked me, scratching a scab on his skinny shin. His eyes had been the pale green of new apples. "What whales?" he'd said.

"The whales down there in the well."

"How'd they fit?"

"Oh," I said then, "they're small whales, just small ones is all, kinda like giant tadpoles. But still whales. Still what you'd call whales," I'd said.

"But," Malcolm had said, looking slanted at me through those long, white lashes, "they'd have to swim 'round and 'round."

"Yes," I'd said. "They do."

After thinking about this a minute or two, he'd said, "Well, they must get mighty dizzy."

And then it had just come to me. Things did then. "That's how they tell the fortunes," I'd told him.

Oh, he'd been surprised at that, but he'd believed me. And the thing is, I had too.

From then on we'd gone to the whales for our fortunes. We'd bring a gift, an empty cicada shell, Grandma's opal hat pin or a last bite of favorite food, and then we'd drop it through the round hole in the cistern cover. We'd whirl around three times on one foot, saying,

> *"Whale whale in the well,*
> *swim around*
> *and tell, tell, tell!"*

Then, quick dropped down on our stomachs, me first, then him, we'd put our eye to the cistern hole, smelling that darkness, that cold, secret wetness. Then we'd turn an ear to the hole to hear our fortune.

And somehow we did.

Or we heard something. Whish of air, maybe. But it seemed like words, you could almost make them out. Or was it just a hollow echo from our own voices coming back to us?

But see, we believed and that made all the difference.

Malcolm believed. I believed.

Now Malcolm believes in nothing at all.

My brother Malcolm with his green apple eyes lives in Chicago and owns thousands of things.

My brother Malcolm told Jack that I'd always been a little crazy. That I had bad blood.

Like her.

But I don't care about Malcolm now. Finally far away from that bed where I lay for seventeen days, I am alive.

I dance around the well. Hey, I'm singing. Hey, hey, hey, loop the loop, um shah widdy, diddle, dingle all the day. I can leap clean across the whales below like a deer.

Above me the tree leaves shwoop in the wind.

I can dance this thing away. I know I can. The bees hum along with me. I make a crown of clover and keep on singing.

Above me now in the tree branches sits a robin redbreast. He cocks his head at me and lets it out. He doesn't belt it like I do but his song's pretty good. No other sound but the branches stretching in the wind and that robin singing, singing, singing.

One night before I left New York I had the strangest dream of Maybelleen and me.

We were sitting on the porch swing where the house used to be and she was telling me that love is never-ending while she pulled out her hair.

I remember it being so hard to watch yet not being able to do anything at all to stop it. Finally she'd looked at me with a bleeding head and said to me, "You don't know the difference between anything at all."

"What?" I'd said to her, but then she was pulling off her arms. "Skin the cat," she'd said.

I remember thinking that this was all crazy. I have to question my mind. But then she was whole again and her hair was just fine. I remember thinking in the dream, nut-brown hair, she has nut-brown hair. "Love circles around and around," she'd said, "it goes like a cat chasing its tail."

I'd reached out then and touched her hand. "Would you like it?" she'd asked me and she'd broken it off clean, like snapping a sugar pea. "Here you keep it."

And I'd sat there on the porch swing with Maybelleen's hand in my lap but it wasn't strange to me then, it was like something finally made sense. And then she'd walked away and the house started blazing but I'd sat there still on the porch swing stroking Maybelleen's hand.

All this day I've been in that Texas jail cell thinking about that—her giving me her hand.

What did she think about in that Texas jail cell while she waited for them to hang her?

DAY THREE

If you sleep in a hayloft naked you will not rest. Hay is not soft but bristles like a mad dog. It pokes you in the cheek, the breast, in every tender place. I have to wrap up in a coat with my purse under my head to finally fall asleep. This morning my body aches and moans and I feel nothing but confusion about where I am and where to go.

When I'd heard about the house exploding Jack and I were living in New York and we were happy. The day I got the letter from the lawyer I'd just laid there on the bed, on my grandmother's handmade quilt, and picked off the corn-flowers. I'd picked off each careful blue flower that my grandmother had made by hand, twisting blue cotton into the shape of a flower, looping it 'round and 'round with thread, and then sewn with infinite patience onto the quilt. There were more than a hundred blue flowers on the quilt.

I'd picked them all off. I remember this now, sitting in the hayloft with my grandmother Ivy rocketed off to heaven and me left with that naked quilt.

I keep remembering everything. I think it's the smells that do it. The air brings the odor of memories.

I walk through the barnyard but that living scent of manure is gone. Not even the ghost of a Banty rooster struts this barnyard now.

I get a thick stick and poke around awhile at the edge of the pit where the house once stood. I don't know what I'm looking for, a piece of china, a half-burned picture of someone, a twisted gold ring, something, anything.

But it's just dirt, dirt, and more dirt. Weeds too, growing here and there where the sun hits, and I know that the hole's been getting even smaller all the years I've been gone, all the years Grandma and Grandpa have been gone. It rains and more earth falls down into the hole until eventually it will be all filled in, then covered with brambles and more weeds and you won't even know that there was once a house here or a heart or even a hope.

Not even a house to haunt.

It'll just become a site for someone to discover and plow over.

There won't be any history left at all.

I throw that stick as far away as I can.

DAY FOUR

I smell. I smell like spent ground. I dreamed of Maybelleen again last night.

I watch the red-winged blackbirds fighting on the barbed-wire fence.

I can't see the hole from here and that's a good thing for me. From my purse I pull out my two photographs, one of Jack playing his guitar downtown, his face twisted with joy, more twisted with joy than when we ever did anything—even make love. The other one of Maybelleen taken a few days before they hanged her in Mud Creek, Texas.

She stands there looking almost bored, the missionaries on either side, one simpering for the camera like a girl at a Sunday-school picnic and the other looking up, probably for a sign from heaven.

Maybelleen stares straight at the camera like she doesn't give a damn.

I stare at my arm. At the veins running blue. Her blood's in me but I can't find it.

I was always even afraid of the dark.

This afternoon I went to the well.

All I had to give for my fortune was my wedding band. I dropped it in and turned my head. All I heard was a thin

27

splash as it hit the water far below. There wasn't an echo of anything at all.

And no matter how hard I try, I can't remember the dream I had.

Everything goes in a straight line says mathematics. Point A goes to point B. But my line always curves and jigs.

Maybelleen has something to say.

I just can't seem to hear and it seems as though the sun's gone out in the middle of the day. I need to make a connection. And I'm clean worn out from dancing. I haven't got even a song in me.

The bees have all gone away. The hay has turned from green to dust. I've fooled myself. Home, home, home. Torn-up earth and dead whales is what there is. I'd wish for a tear, but my wishes are long used up.

If I knew more about math I might figure out a straight line. But I never paid much attention. Never thought I'd have to.

DAY FIVE

Jefferson County Sheriff's Office
To Serve and Protect

"What the hell happened up there, Jim? Sam Fredericks was in here, sayin' they found her swingin' and turnin' blue."

The county sheriff stood up from his desk as his deputy, a thirty-four-year-old sometime farmer, leaned back against the cracked, yellow wall.

The deputy ran his fingers through his hair and said, "Damned if I know really."

"I got a call from Tom Harris said he found Ivy Dye's grandkid up there in the barn, hanged and naked," said the sheriff. "That's something. Clevon Ludmiller shot himself in the head last year, but I don't remember a hanging 'round here for years."

"Nope," said the deputy, pulling out a form from the desk.

"Damn," said the sheriff. "That's the one ran up to New York, ain't it? Naked. I swear."

"He'd cut her down," said his deputy. "She musta just done it when Tom got there. He come up the ladder and she was choking and swinging he said, back and forth like she'd given herself a kick-start off a pile of baled hay." The deputy pulled at his hair. "I saw her lying there," he went on. "She looked right at me, I swear she did, though a second later she shut her eyes."

"Lucky thing he'd gone up there to get some cow feed or she'd be six feet under," said the sheriff. "Good thing he's got an eye on that farm."

The deputy poured a cup of coffee and sat down at the metal desk. "When the ambulance came, she kept starin' at me," he said to the sheriff, "tryin' to talk and just starin' at me. Her eyes were bulging out in a strange way." He tapped a pen on the wood desk and ran his hand through his hair again.

The sheriff put on his wide-brimmed hat and said, "They say that happens when you get hung, your eyeballs poke out, sometimes I heard they even pop right out of the head. I can't say I understand, Jim, what it is that gets people to that point where they go flyin' off the handle and pull this kinda stunt. But you know, them folks was always kinda strange, been in this county for years and years and don't hardly anyone know much about 'em. Now, I do know that old gal way back, Maybelleen. She got hung. Got hung down in Texas. Now, Maybelleen MacGregor was Ivy Dye's sister and I remember my mama talkin' about her, she knew them folks pretty well. That Maybelleen ran off with some other gal's man and she got herself hung for armed robbery way back, way back before the First World War. Remember hearin' about that, Jim? My mama told me that was some kind of scandal all them years ago. That was Maybelleen. The outlaw. Right up there with Annie Oakley. Famous. She was pretty famous. Don't think her folks appreciated it, though."

"Sure. Maybelleen." The deputy stared down at the blank forms in front of him. "I guess I got to put down attempted suicide here where it says Give Reason For Call."

"Well, that's what it was wasn't it?"

"I'm not sure," said the deputy.

"What the hell do you mean, Jim? Whaddaya call it when you find someone swinging from a rope in a hayloft? Wasn't attempted murder was it? Think Tom Harris went up there and strung her up?"

"No."

The sheriff laughed. The deputy twisted the pen through his fingers.

"Well, fill that damn thing in so's we can file it and let's get us some lunch. I feel like that chopped steak today, love that mushroom gravy." The sheriff sucked in his stomach and turned his profile to the deputy.

"Think I'm losin' any weight, Jim?"

The deputy didn't answer. He was watching a fly climb up the windowpane.

"Look, Jim, some people are just crazy, it's in the family, runs in it, you know. Still you just don't know how a body could wanna throw it all away.

"Damn! Look now! It's started rainin'. I was goin' fishin' with Will this afternoon. Guess that's off. That means I'm gonna have to go home and play twenty questions with Susie. Oh, you can bet your bottom dollar she'll know more about this damn thing than the both of us. She's probably already been on the phone with the girl's aunt over in Bumbleboro."

The sheriff turned to the deputy and slapped his shoulder. "Hey, now, come on, Jim. You don't know the girl. It's sad and all. But her people are with her now. The hospital got ahold of her aunt and uncle up to Bumbleboro. It's sad and I know it."

The sheriff tapped the windowpane and the fly circled and landed on his shoulder.

"Purple Jesus! Damn this rain. Nothin' but trash fish in the rain."

"Well, you just don't know about people sometimes," said the deputy, "you just don't know what kinda pain they're in."

"What? Well let's get us some lunch," said the sheriff. "I know what kinda pain this empty stomach's in."

The sheriff laughed and the deputy filled out the form. But he couldn't eat and he couldn't get the woman's face out of his mind.

Maybelleen

On the New Mexico Border

In 1902 the buffalo were dead, stacked to heaven. At the base of the Sacramento Mountains a young man, eighteen or nineteen, and a thirty-seven-year-old woman who gave too much thought to dying, stretched out on wool blankets under the black sky.

"I love you," the young man said, but the woman said, "Hush" and "Listen." The wind circled and rattled the cottonwoods. The sound was like the click of bones.

"There's nothin'," said the young man and pulled the woman to him. He held her. He felt her heartbeat through his flannel shirt and he put his ear to her breast and listened.

Inside her he heard the thick liquid of her body; the

coming and going of her blood and the communication of her bowels. He felt the thin whiteness of her ribs and was amazed. He kept trying to pull her back to the world. But she kept pulling away.

"It don't matter no more," he said to her heart. "None of 'em matter. They run off and they ain't comin' back 'cause they're skeered as rats and that's just what they are. Skeered rats."

She stroked his hair and smiled.

"I love you, May." He fell asleep.

She laid her Smith & Wesson at first between them, then picked it up and moved it to her side.

For a while she looked up at the stars. "Orion," she said out loud but he was out cold, cuddled up to her, with an arm around her neck. The stars were different now that Bill was dead. It seemed they'd moved just the tiniest bit but she didn't have anyone to ask if it were true.

She began to half dream of buffalo, like she used to do, of huge snorting brown bulls, breath hanging white in the winter air. She dreamed the thunder of them racing in an enormous single will across plains that tilted under their weight.

Buffalo dreams mean something mighty, Bill had told her. Dreams of buffalo are dreams of power and death. Bill's grandmother had told him all about buffalo dreams. She'd been Pawnee, he'd told her once. Sioux, he'd told her another time.

He'd seen the bones, he'd said, when they were white mountains. He said there had been bones for hundreds of miles.

"For every hundred buffalo I'll kill one of them what killed 'em," he'd told her. And by the time they shot him back of the shack in Chandler, Oklahoma, he'd shot at least five men. Might have been one among them who'd shot a buffalo or two. But probably not. Even then the buffalo had long been gone.

But she was the one who dreamed of them.

Her buffalo dreams had come always unexpected, when she was exhausted after riding all day, when they put up outside Santa Fe or stayed with friends in Caddo or Choctaw City. One time she'd dreamed them shivering in a cave while they waited for spring so they could ride again.

She'd always wake up in a cold sweat still smelling the rankness of their skin. And she'd always tell Bill about her dream.

One night he'd pushed her against a wall with his hand on her neck and his breath hot with whiskey. It was the only time she ever saw him drink.

"I didn't kill the buffalo," she'd said to Bill then, looking straight into his dark eyes. He'd had eyes so black you couldn't find the pupil.

He'd fallen to the ground and hugged himself as if he were cold.

Bill couldn't figure out why she had the dreams that he thought should be his. But ever after he'd asked her time and again, "Did you have the dream?"

She'd tell him: "Bill, last night I dreamed again that I was dead and I was lying alone in a huge sea of high grass. The grass was cold with dew and I knew it was just before morning. I could see myself in the dream, I looked at it from the outside and even though I didn't look like me, I knew that it was. I was painted, Bill. I was painted in black and white and I was waiting for something.

"In the dream I saw the sun come up but it didn't get any warmer and I couldn't move although the sun was high overhead.

"Then Bill, there came a buffalo, a huge brown bull and his head was as big as a barn door. He had giant eyes, Bill, so large I might have crawled inside them and curled up. That's what I wanted to do in this dream, crawl into the eye of the buffalo and be carried away inside him.

"But then he blew on me, Bill, this buffalo did, and his breath? Why, honey, it smelled of sweet chewed-up flowers and green summer grass. And then I could stand.

"And he was so big, big as, as, a railroad car, that's how big he was. But then, see, I found I could climb right up on him and stand on his back. So I climbed him like a child climbing rocks and from up there I could see for thousands of miles.

"I could see Philadelphia and Boston, Kansas City and Fort Worth. I could see way off to New York City.

"But when I looked down I saw that the high grass where I'd been lying was only a tiny, small patch, no bigger than a little wild yard out back of somebody's house.

"But I could feel the buffalo under me, the moving of his muscles and I knew he wanted to walk but there was nowhere to go, and so we stood there, the buffalo and me, in the little patch of grass and that's all."

Bill had grabbed her face then, and he'd been sickly pale. "Who are you?" he'd asked her. "Who are you?"

She'd just looked at him then and loved him all the more. "You know who I am, Bill," she'd said and he'd turned away from her.

Then he'd turned back and he'd been excited. He'd waved his arms in the air as if pulling in a vision. "Oh, oh," he'd said. "I see it now. It means something, May. It means something mighty. I'll have to think on it."

And he'd climbed up on the mesa then and sat under the sky waiting to find the meaning in her dream. Bill looked for meaning in everything.

Now just as her buffalo dream was starting the boy started shaking her awake. "We gotta get goin', May," he said.

She'd said, "Not yet."

But he told her it was coming on dawn and she knew he

was right. With Vitus and Shoe gone they were less visible but more vulnerable too. If they didn't head south fast they'd be trapped in Texas and they wanted to make Jiminez fast before they lost a chance at all.

Bill had only been gone a week and she was living that half-life you live when you're partly dead. She wanted to get across the border, pay the money. Buy that town.

This boy loved and loved her. Once or twice when she'd let him touch her and run his hands all over her, the look on his face had almost made her laugh out loud.

Hanging wasn't anything she was particularly looking forward to, but outlawing wasn't much without Bill. She shook the thought away, picked up her Smith & Wesson, and pulled the bag out from under her head.

Twenty thousand in gold. Enough to buy that town in Mexico. For the Indians. For Bill's Indians.

They weren't going to get her before she did what she could. Even if everyone else in the world thought it was a stupid idea. It was at the least, an honest idea, thought up with humanity. She couldn't think of much else worth dying for.

"That's what it means, May!" He'd been all in a fever. He'd come to her while she was deep asleep and he'd shaken her until she woke. "It means we got to make a new nation! A new nation for the People!"

"What people?" she'd asked. Her head had been syrupy with sleep.

"For the Indians! Don't you see? That's what the dream says. Build a new nation! We'll build a new nation, we'll tell them to come. That's what it means. I'll tell them, the Brules, the Paiutes, all the tribes. All they need's a place to start over. My People."

He'd stood there on the rock and proclaimed it to them all.

We must go to a new country. We must build a new nation. No more dirt eating.

He'd laughed and kissed her. "Alright, Bill," she'd said and she'd begun laughing too. "We will."

"Who you think you are?" Young Pup had said then. "Moses?"

"A promised land! That's right!" Bill had said. He'd tapped the boy's head and smiled. Pup had ducked his head and said, "Moses. Thought we were in the bank robbin' business."

"There ain't no business to robbin' if you ain't givin' it back again. You got to find some meanin', Pup, or you might as well just lay down now."

"There ain't no meanin'," the boy had replied. "That's the joke."

Now again here he was, that same boy, sayin', "Come on, come on. We gotta get going."

"You hated Bill, didn't you?" She stared at him, at those gray eyes. "All that time you just wanted him dead."

"I love you," was all he'd said.

So she got up. They saddled the horses, gave them water,

and headed down past Amarillo, going east around El Paso. They figured to dart quick over the Mexican border because they knew Rangers were out hunting for them. And others too.

She had never dreamed of this ever, while she'd filled up empty days with books and fine embroidery in Kentucky, that one day she'd have a price on her head. In those days she'd dreamed of Ceylonese tea and the mountains of Borneo. Never had she dreamed of prairie storms and deserts, of scorpions and flat blank land. In her most fevered dreams, and she'd gotten hot with a few, never ever did she see herself with a bag of gold, heading for somewhere to do something so crazy. Never had she thought she'd be alive and dead all at once.

But this was no dream. She was the outlaw Maybelleen MacGregor, and she was riding with Stuart Ray Colvin—the one they'd come to call Young Pup. The two left who'd ridden with Mexican Bill. Once again, she said to the boy, "I still don't see why Vitus and Shoe would run off."

"It figures," he said. "They were low-bellied cowards."

"Still, I can hardly believe it." Because she couldn't. But then, she had to. They were all alone. And so ridiculous too. A schoolteacher from Kentucky and a green boy, really thinking they could do this thing all by themselves. She shook her head and climbed up on Dr. Brown's mare, Pup got up on Bill's horse, a strong, red, ugly thing. They rode side by side.

That morning right before they'd left, Pup named the horse because Bill never had. He named the horse Lucky Dollar because it made Maybelleen laugh.

Then he sang her songs as they rode toward the border. "In 1814 we took a little trip, along with Colonel Jackson down the mighty Mississip, oh, we took a little bacon and we . . ."

She'd buy a place with the gold and tell the Indians to come. Maybe if she told them about her dream they really would come. Then they could hang her.

Still she found herself thinking again, if she hadn't been so empty she might have had a child. But it was just too bad. She was hollow as a fallen log.

"Oh we fired our guns but the British kept acomin' . . ."

Margaret

Hospital

It was hard to look at her. Tied up like that with tubes and her neck raw and her eyes closed and she so small in the middle of those things that twisted like vines all around her.

The deputy turned his hat around in his hands. The aunt and uncle sat side by side on wooden chairs next to the bed.

Her face was puffy as though it was made of clouds.

"It was good of you to stop by," the aunt said. "She's doing better now. They say there's no brain damage and that's really a miracle. She just sleeps all the time."

He couldn't say anything but watched her breathing.

"We'll have her home in a week or two."

He'd just nodded and left. Two days later he would come back and do the same thing again. Just look.

The first time she opened her eyes she'd said, "Where is he?"

No one knew who she was talking about.

But she kept on saying that she'd dreamed this angel, that she'd seen him true. Her aunt held her when she tossed around and threw pillows to the floor. She'd said, "I saw an angel but I couldn't tell."

"Tell what?" asked her uncle, picking up pillows from the floor.

"If he was taking me or leaving me."

Then the doctor came and put her back to sleep for a long time.

Maybelleen

Captured

And was it really anything at all if she slept with him? If he touched her body? She felt nothing. She was dead already. And if there was something that came out of her, something like a moan or nearly a scream, if her cells reacted, was that anything at all?

Did she notice him really? He was just a child but he looked at her too sharp, too piercing. As though he really understood something. Or, as if he wanted to understand so badly that it made him out of kilter, all akimbo. Even in her half existence she recognized something oozing from him in too great a strength. Too great for a body or a boy to handle. Too much.

One time when she'd said I love you back, she had meant it for someone else.

She'd felt his comprehension in the way he pushed inside her. She felt his anger, then she felt his fear. His hurt didn't touch her though. She just got up and got dressed. All around the coyotes laughed.

She wanted to say she was sorry but she didn't.

So they rode on and on and she could feel his hate squeezing at her back. She didn't care. Hollow as a log was she. The things of this world were behind her now.

But even in her dead dream life she could see that love had walked the boy around a corner where he'd smacked right into hate.

Now he hated her and hated her and it was only a matter of time. Now she sang and he followed her glumly on the red horse, his face set, his gray eyes gone wild.

She knew what she'd done. Though it hadn't been on purpose. He'd walked right into the opportunity. Now it was out of her hands. She laughed too high, too thin. He stared at the horizon, his love twisting inside him like a thorny vine.

How thin that thread, thought Maybelleen. That thread between it all; birth, death, love, and bile.

It was only a matter of time. She was too tired of thinking.

~∙ℬ℧

She wasn't surprised to find they were being followed. she thought it kind of funny that it was so easy to pick up their traces. She'd only spent a year with Bill, really knew nothing about tracking, or wind smells, but she knew immediately when they were behind them. She could nearly read their minds. Pup would look at her odd, his eyes gone cold and cloudy, a winter storm ready to break. He knew they were there too.

He was frightened. She could smell it.

She didn't care.

Two men. Two tall thin men on big horses. Government horses followed them for a day and night through the canyons and though they only stopped to water the horses and let them blow and get their wind, they both knew it was only a matter of time.

Finally, the afternoon of the second day, the sun was hot. Maybelleen sweated in Bill's blue shirt. She could smell herself. They were stopped by a tiny creek, water through mud, really. Her mare was blowing, its ribs bellowing beneath the saddle. She pulled the bridle toward the little water pool and as the mare drank, she stooped on her haunches and threw some of the brackish water on her face.

"May," she heard.

When she turned, Pup had her gun and his both, trained at her head.

"Yes," she'd said. "What is it?"

"You know," he'd said.

"So this," she'd said, "is it?"

"Shut up. I want you to take off your clothes, May."

So she had. She'd taken off her clothes and the sun had banged into her. She felt all the white places hit by the sun changing and growing hot. She didn't cover herself with her arms. Didn't hide her breast or belly. She stood there in front of the boy naked, her feet in mud, waiting.

"So," he'd said. "You see, you do what I say and you won't ever get hurt."

"Won't ever?" she'd said, looking him in the face.

"I always said so," he'd said then, standing there only eighteen and feeling his hate melting with the tears that were coming. "Oh, May," he'd said. He'd covered his face then, his nose was beginning to run. "I only loved you the best and the sweetest." He raised his head and pointed the guns again at her. "I'm easy to love, don't you see?"

"I see." The mare snorted behind her.

"That's all you have to do then," he said. "Just say. Just say it to me."

But she was frozen in the sun and trapped in mud.

And anyway, she was a ghost.

"Oh, May!" he'd sobbed.

47

"What happened to Shoe and Vitus?" That's what she'd finally said. "What really happened?"

He'd looked at her and his lip had curled in a smile gone bad. She'd felt herself begin to shake, begin to feel. Out of her mouth an ooooh had come and she'd trembled from the inside out.

And then one of the men who'd tracked them came over the rise to the creek. His face had been hidden in the shadow of his big lawman hat. He held a rifle close to his cheek. Maybelleen, naked, sun-kissed, stood as marble as the boy had turned the guns away from her and fired first from one and then from the other. She watched the man standing there, forty feet away, his hat blown off with the top of his head, register first surprise and then the comprehension of death. As he fell, she'd turned her head and watched the boy as he came around behind her. She never moved more than the muscles of her neck as she followed him with her eyes. He lifted the saddlebag from her mare. The bag heavy with Bill's dream, and their eyes still locked together, forever it seemed, he threw it across the back of the mean, red horse, Bill's horse.

They stared at each other. She said nothing.

Neither did he. He kicked the horse hard, then lashed with the reins. Left her standing naked in the mud with the sun raining down, pelting her with hotness.

As she turned her head away from the sound of his flight,

she'd heard a moaning across the creek where the Ranger lay dying.

She sat down in the water and the mud. Her mare nuzzled her hair and blew into it with sweet animal breath.

That was how the other Ranger found her. That's how Maybelleen was captured.

Margaret

Looking at Angles

I don't remember those thirty-two days. Aunt Opal says that's how long I was in the hospital but I can't remember.

That's alright, Aunt Opal says, because I'm with family now. But it isn't. It isn't alright not to remember a month.

On Thursdays now—so many have passed—Aunt Opal and Uncle Wendell drive me to the doctor in Louisville. The head doctor.

Depression, he tells me in a quiet serious voice. Exhaustion. Take these in the morning, take that at night.

This is for laughter. This is for tears.

Is it in the family? That's what he asked.

Does it run straight in a line from one to another?

But of course you aren't crazy, just worn-out. Just tired. Aunt Opal and Uncle Wendell have taken me in like their own.

Look at Tom, they say. That's their boy. Never married, never will, being fifty by now. Only thing he cares about is drinking and fishing.

You're our girl, Margaret. You're our girl now.

Take this in the morning, take that at night.

Bigger and smaller, dark and light.

I laugh. I have to. Just because I tried to hang myself doesn't mean a thing. I'm certainly not strapping on a six-shooter and riding off to the open range. I'm not developing into a legend.

Because she was. Maybelleen was.

Maybe you don't read about her as much as the others, but she was something. Sometimes I wonder if that's why you don't hardly ever hear anything about her. Belle Starr became an American legend and Bonnie Parker.

Maybelleen got swept under the rug.

Just crazy, they decided. Plain nut.

"Honey," says Aunt Opal the other night, "what about the farm? What do you plan to do? Tom's been looking after it but it's just sitting there going to waste. You ought to do something with that farm, honey, Ivy wanted you to. How about building a little house out there?"

Here in Bumbleboro the time goes by gently, or perhaps

I'm gently going with time. When Malcolm and I used to come out here to see Aunt Opal and Uncle Wendell in Grandpa's DeSoto, we used to sit in the backseat and say over and over, "Where you goin'? Bumbleboro? Hey that's a buzzin' place!"

Then we'd laugh like idiots.

Malcolm. He went straight from point A to B.

I'm stuck here in the middle of the alphabet.

I spend most of my time in the spare room, lying on the peach-colored comforter drifting gently along with all this time. Time flows like water now. It doesn't seem like anything has to hurry anymore.

Aunt Opal tries, she comes up and sits in the rocker and talks and talks. She brings me photographs.

"Here, there's Ivy and me before she married your grandpa. She was something to see. I wasn't too bad myself. Before your grandma told this whole town to go to hell, she was the most popular girl in the county. Now, here's you children on Christmas in 1939."

I look at the pictures and they're so flat. There's nothing there of me.

Uncle Wendell will come by sometimes and show me his lures, bluebottle and night crawler, all made by hand.

They're good to me and I guess I fill in some gap for them.

But I heard them late that night when they first brought me here to the peach-colored room.

Aunt Opal crying. "Why didn't she let us know she'd come home? Why'd she do that? Why'd she do that?"

"She's always been that way, Opal, you know that. You remember what Ivy said. Flair for drama. Hung up on you know who. But you gotta think, Opal, what it was like for them children with not even a memory of their poor dead parents and raised up over there at the farm with two old folks."

"They weren't that old, Wendell. They did the best they could. It's not right, Wendell, I swear. Sometimes I think it'd do her a world of good to know the truth."

"Stop that, Opal!" said Uncle Wendell. "That decision had nothing to do with you. She doesn't need hearing any of that from you. You hear me?"

I lay there surrounded by the pale shadows of the room, hearing the katydids going out the window, the eerie music they play, hearing them pulling Maybelleen in closer and closer. Aunt Opal and Uncle Wendell look at me and I see them through my eyelashes. They think I'm asleep.

"I never had a girl. I know Ivy just fell in love with her," she whispers. "And she was such a pretty little thing."

"You wanted her here, woman," he'd said.

Then the door had slammed.

I know what they're thinking though. I'm just like her, just like her.

But that isn't true. I've never done a thing in my life.

In my dream, she gave me her hand. She was capable of decisions.

I keep waiting and waiting for another sign.

One day a week ago I was sitting in the kitchen with Aunt Opal. But she's not really my aunt at all. She's my grandmother's first cousin, but of course we always called her Aunt.

After Maybelleen left, Aunt Opal was my grandmother's only friend. My grandmother told me that. Maybelleen scandalized everyone, the way she ran off with another woman's man. Nobody would socialize with Ivy MacGregor after that. After my grandma Ivy told them to all go to hell.

The radio's playing something funny, music like a cartoon and Aunt Opal is telling me about the cabinets and cherry brandy.

"See that cherry tree out there? You would not believe the cherries we get from that tree! It's amazing! Last year I made cherry pies and cherry pies and still more cherries! So. I make cherry jelly and cherry bread and Wendell's moanin' from all those cherries in his gelatin and cherries in his flapjacks, so I get an idea that I might make some cherry brandy, so I do, but I don't tell Wendell on account of he can't drink at all . . ."

I concentrate on the music, its absurd swells and punctuations.

"And I never let him near any kind of liquor on account of his ulcerated stomach he got over there in France in the first war and all."

And Aunt Opal just keeps talking because she's afraid to be quiet with me. She's afraid if she doesn't talk constantly I might pick up a fork and stab myself in the heart.

She doesn't understand that I don't even want to bother. I keep smiling at her as much as I can. I nod frequently.

"So I had these new cabinets put in. Yellow. I was thinking it was too much, too bright and all, but now I like them. Do you like them, Margaret? Yes, well. Anyway, I put that cherry brandy up in the tip-top of this new cabinet here."

She tapped a bright yellow cabinet door. "I'm seventy-five and Wendell's eighty last year. I figure there's no possible way he's going to find that cherry brandy up on that top shelf of that cabinet. Folks our age don't go climbing around lookin' on top shelves."

While she's talking, going on about how Uncle Wendell sniffs out that cherry brandy and guess what?—gets plastered, I began to hear the faintest rustling in the corner of the kitchen, right by the screen door.

Something's stirring there like a wind gathering leaves and as I watch I see something, I'm sure I do, but I don't know what it is.

I dream of Maybelleen all the time now and I think it might be her, trying to break through, to come through to me here and Aunt Opal's going on, "He had such a stomachache for a week! Had to get the doctor and all and . . ."

But try as hard as I can, I can see nothing in the corner by the screen door and the rustling sound quiets down like the wind after rain.

But these are surely signs.

Yesterday that man came. The sheriff's deputy.

I knew he would.

I was watching the way evening light changed the pattern of the peach wallpaper when Aunt Opal called to me from downstairs.

"Margaret, honey, you've got a caller."

But in that certain light, just before the sun falls, you begin to pick things out in the wallpaper. Faces. You begin to see that they've always been there all along and it just takes the right light to bring them out.

I'm lying there stretched out in my blue house robe, not even stockings on, when she opens the door and pokes in her head.

"Margaret," she says, "here's Jim O'Toole come to see how you're doing." And she swings the door wide and just lets him in.

He doesn't say anything. I don't say anything. Aunt Opal stands behind him with a fool grin on her face. Something falls heavy on my chest, *bang*. Like a fist came at me and stopped my heart.

I remember him so much clearer than I'd thought. He saw me right after. He was there.

"I just thought I'd check and see how you're feeling."

"She's feeling fine, now. Just a little accident, she's worn out, Jim, you don't know. She was up in New York too long and she went through too much. But she's feeling much better now. Now that she's home again. Aren't you honey?"

"Yes," I said.

We stared at each other. His name is Jim.

"Well," he said. He put the hat on he'd been holding in his hands. He was wearing a white shirt and brown pants. His eyes slant up at the corners and are black. "I just wanted to check," he said. And he left.

Today I ask Aunt Opal if she has family pictures, old ones.

"Of Ivy?" she says. "I've got old reunion pictures you'd probably love to see."

"No," I say, "Maybelleen."

She brushes her hands on her apron a dozen times and looks at me. "Maybe," she says. "I might."

She says she'll look after supper for a box in the back of the closet. She has a box of a few of Ivy's things she says.

The phone rings and somehow I know it's that man. These days I know all the wrong things.

I don't like it. When Aunt Opal hands me the phone I can't make hardly any sense at all of what he's saying. But actually he doesn't say much, its just that I can't really make heads or tails of it.

"Well?" says Aunt Opal when I hang up.

"He's taking me to the movies in Louisville Saturday."

"That's wonderful!" she says. "Let's make some pudding. Wendell loves chocolate pudding though it's bad for his teeth. You know half those aren't his real teeth and what a time I had getting him to get those teeth of his fitted right."

I suddenly realize it's the end of October. I left New York in June.

"But that's fine," says Aunt Opal, "you got to take all you can before it's too late."

I haven't been able to find my wedding ring. I've looked everywhere. Jack has never called or written, and of course, he must know I'm here.

Why ever did I tell that man I would go?

Maybelleen
1899
Kentucky

How many days, she wondered, as she threaded another needle, would it take to get to San Francisco—now that they'd built the railroad clean out to California.

"May, you seen that biscuit tin? The Chinese one?" Her sister's voice seemed far away although she was only next door in the pantry. "I want to take some of those lovely cookies you baked to the tea. I don't think I've made enough of this gingerbread."

I think it said three days in the magazine. She bit the end off the thread. Only three days. From the kitchen she could smell the gingerbread. The odor of cinnamon and cloves became a vision of deserts and date palms.

"May, honey, you hear me? We used it—ouch! May! Everything's falling out of this cabinet! Honey, can you come here? May? May!"

"I'm coming." Maybelleen stood up and looked at herself in the pier glass in the powder room where she'd been embroidering all morning. The pillowcase she'd worked on was tossed aside on the floor. "I'm not pretty," she said to the glass. "I'm not young and not pretty."

In the pantry Ivy stood surrounded by baskets and biscuit tins that had fallen out of the cupboard. "May, I can't find that Chinese tin we had for Christmas last year. I want to use that one for the cookies. I don't know what to do, everything is out of order and everything is just, oh! it's just too much. You know how Elizabeth Barrymore is. You know just how she is! We can't bring the cookies in an old dented tin, we just can't!"

Ivy sat down on an old ladderback chair and began to cry.

"May, please find that tin! Elizabeth has hated me ever since Sam Dye proposed and you know that. I can't take just any old tin to her fancy tea party!"

Maybelleen stood for a moment in the doorway. Her sister was wiping her face with her apron and sniffling. "It isn't my fault that Eliza Barrymore is ugly as a monkey."

Ivy looked up at Maybelleen, tears clouding her hazel eyes.

Crying only makes her skin more beautiful, thought Maybelleen. Ivy wiped her nose on her apron. "Do you think Mama would let me borrow her jet earrings?"

"Do you ever think about anything, Ivy?" asked Maybelleen.

"What do you mean, May? Of course I do. What a stupid thing to say! Why are you staring at me? I can't help it, I'm nervous going over to the Barrymores."

"Then why don't you just stay home?"

"What? And have Eliza Barrymore saying I don't have the nerve to come? Oh, you mean because it's a literary thing? Well, I read that book. Yes I did! And I'd rather die, that's all! I'd just rather die!"

Maybelleen shrugged her shoulders and turned away. Or Mexico, she thought. Parrots in the trees and the sound of running water off high cliff walls. Paris, Brussels, Chicago, anywhere.

"May! Where are you going? What's wrong with you anymore?"

Maybelleen passed through the dining room. The china cabinet stood exactly where it had stood since she was a child. The black walnut sideboard was against the east wall and the dining table sat squarely in the middle of the room. The table shone from a thousand applications of beeswax.

"Nothing has ever changed," she said to herself.

"May, please help me find it." But Maybelleen ignored her.

She heard her sister throwing things around in the pantry. The sounds clattered about her as she stood staring at the dining room. Now, if she took the crystal vase off the sideboard and hid it in the closet, how long would it take them to notice?

"Maybelleen MacGregor, you are being just positively hateful! Ooooh, everyone hates me just because I'm getting married!"

And Maybelleen went up to her room to dress for the first meeting of the Bumbleboro Ladies Literary Society. Before she dressed she took out the sherry from the wardrobe and poured herself a crystal glassful.

She stood at the window while she sipped looking out at the pasture to where it met up with the sky.

There's got to be more, she thought. And she poured another, just a little bit, and found she'd bitten her lip clean through.

They drove the trap. "I wish we had a buggy, May. Or one of those new things. Even though I think they are a little too much, don't you think it'd be fun? People have them everywhere now! Well, maybe not around here. But Tom Francis has one ordered, he says. He'll take us for rides to Louisville.

"What do you think of this pink and gray? Is it alright?"

"It's fine, honey," said Maybelleen. "You look beautiful as always."

"You look pretty too, May, that green suits you. Oh! You found Mama's parrot pin! That's just perfect, honey. Let me tuck in your hair there. May! Don't! Let me just fix it, sugar, it's all falling down. You always let your hair fall down. Was Mama sleeping when we left?"

Maybelleen nodded and pulled her head away from her sister's fingers.

They rode in silence past whitewashed fence posts. The lilacs were in full bloom. The sun skirted behind big white clouds and popped out again. The puddles in the road exploded in arcs on either side of the wheels as they passed.

Ivy took Maybelleen's arm and leaned against her. "You know, I like the way you drive much better than Daddy did. He always made me nervous with that whip and all. You're so relaxed and you know Milk likes you better. How old do you think Milk is now?"

"Oh, about fifteen," said Maybelleen. The big horse tilted his ears toward them at the sound of his name.

"Look," said Ivy, "look how he knows his name! Oh, I don't want him to die, May. Do you think he'll still live a long time?"

"He'll live as long as he wants to, I suppose."

"May, why you being so ornery? Is it Loren? I know he's going to ask you by Fourth of July. I just know it, May."

"I don't care if he does, Ivy."

"Maybelleen! What do you mean? Of course you care!"

Maybelleen didn't answer. They rode the last four miles again in silence to the outskirts of town. Three blocks from the Barrymore's, Ivy pointed to a pale blue house. "That's the house I want. Sam doesn't see the need to move all the way over to Louisville, but then the lovely part is it's only an hour when you need to shop. Of course all his patients will be right here." She took her sister's arm again. "You can always live with us, May. You know Sam would be tickled pink to have you and you could teach our babies, wouldn't that be wonderful? Everyone says you're the best teacher in the world. Don't shake your head at me, miss! At least the best in all Kentucky. May, honey, I don't know what I'd do without you." Ivy put an arm around Maybelleen's waist and kissed her. "But then again, May, you know I'm always stupid and selfish. Of course you never want to leave Mama alone on the farm."

Maybelleen laughed and kissed her sister's cheek. She flicked the whip hard and high above the horse's ears.

The crack it made did not give her half enough satisfaction.

She was thirty-four years old. At the corners of her eyes the lines were etching themselves into open fans. Her teeth were large. She was self-conscious of her big teeth. She had a very long neck and her hands were beginning to show thick, aqua veins.

She was wearing a bright green suit with turquoise boots. She'd worn the boots because they made her think of places where colors jumped and jangled. Now among the other women, the colors she'd chosen startled her and made her feel too large for the dainty pickle forks and compote spoons.

Their hostess greeted them in the parlor where knots of ladies were clustered around floral ottomans and damask-covered chairs. The heavy grape draperies were drawn back and the windows thrown open. Maybelleen tilted her head away from the direct light as Eliza Barrymore took her hand.

"May, you look lovely. I'm so glad to have you. We need an educated woman among us silly flibbertigibbets for an afternoon like this in our little town. I sometimes don't know what possesses me to think that I might have an artistic bone in my body."

"It's a wonderful idea, Eliza." Maybelleen squinted at the woman. The sunlight was hitting her directly in the eyes.

"And here's Ivy, come here honey, and meet my cousin from Chicago. He's kindly deigned to speak to us about the Indians.

"I know I had you all wade through Milton, but it just turned out that our literary society may turn out to be something even more grand. So you see I've even managed a legitimate speaker for our first meeting and poor Milton will just have to dawdle in his purgatory a little bit longer!"

Eliza Barrymore took Ivy's hand. Ivy turned to look at her sister. "Go on, Ivy," said Maybelleen.

Ivy's head tilted toward the hostess and with a sunburst smile she said, "Oh, Eliza, I'm so glad to see you, I've been meaning to call but Mama's been down with a cold."

Eliza Barrymore drew Ivy away. Maybelleen listened as her sister continued, "I'd been thinking all week about asking you about how you made those pickled peaches last summer, they were such a hit, you know . . ."

Maybelleen moved across the parlor, little smiles greeting her here and there until she arrived at the piano. She looked through a book of Schumann and tried to focus on what the black dots on the pages were trying to say.

When she looked up for a moment, she saw her sister and two other women speaking animatedly with a tall young man across the room. He stopped speaking momentarily and looked directly at her. He smiled. She immediately looked down again at the Schumann and continued to study a page until a woman she'd known from church interrupted her, chatting of vinegar and all its unknown healing properties. She absorbed herself in this conversation in the same manner as she had the sheet music.

The hostess served China teas; Oolong, Soochow, Paradise Green, tiny sandwiches of celery and dill, a vast array of pickled fruits and vegetables, ripe spring strawberries and cream, and an enormous pink-and-white crabmeat salad.

Ivy's gingerbread was set upon a sterling cake server. Ivy and Elizabeth Barrymore sat by each other on a sofa, picking at the food, smiling and laughing.

While the food was being laid out, Ivy had told Maybelleen that Eliza was marrying her cousin from Chicago.

"Doctor Brown is here to propose, she thinks, May. Isn't it wonderful? Isn't he so very good-looking? She hasn't seen him since she was a little girl and now she says she's fallen in love. He's here to find a wife—his mother wrote to her—a helper in his work with the Indians. Oh, it's so very romantic, May. I wish Sam were just a tiny bit romantic."

When the food was ready, Maybelleen took nothing but tea and the crab salad. She found a chair by the window. She wondered where the crab had come from, although she supposed you could buy anything now. Her mother, being a farmer's wife, had never believed in tinned food.

Maybelleen had only read about crab. People ate it in English novels. She remembered a plate in a book she'd loved as a child, pictures of animals with names exotic; Hippasteria spinosa—the starfish, and Carcinides maenas—the crab.

She decided she would buy some crabmeat the next time she went to Louisville—tins of it. She'd hoard it in a secret place and eat it only when her mother or sister were nowhere about. Then she'd open it up and pull it out of its silver tin with a fork onto a pearl-white plate. She'd exalt in its sea taste, never hearing about cost or the dangers of food poisoning. She ate slowly and stared out the window at daffodils and tulips. All about her voices hummed but she didn't listen and didn't care that she was being ignored. When Dr. Brown sat down on the low stool at her feet, balancing a well-stocked plate on his knee, she didn't even notice.

"I understand your first book was to be *Paradise Lost* but that a number of the ladies found it a bit too much for discussion."

Maybelleen turned her head from the flowers and looked down at the man seated on the ottoman.

"Please excuse the intrusion, Miss MacGregor," he said. "I am Dr. Elias Brown, newly here from Chicago. Your beautiful state has kindly embraced me in my mission of proselytizer and my cousin has graced me with her kind invitation to be a part of your first literary gathering. Oh! But I see that you are in a reverie, were you regretting Milton will not be given audience here today, perhaps?"

Staring at the man who had interrupted her first experience with crab, she couldn't remember for a moment if she'd been introduced to him or not.

"The moaning of lost souls grates on my nerves," was what she said.

It was all she could think of to say. She put her fork down on her plate. She had never been able to eat in front of strangers.

"Then you are not among them?"

"What?"

"The lost souls," said Dr. Brown, smiling at her.

He smoothed his mustache and small white bread crumbs fell like dust.

"I don't moan," said Maybelleen.

She turned back to the window. She had noticed that the man was handsome. This made it very difficult for her to look at him. He had very dark brown hair and a distinct profile. His chin was strong, she noted before she turned away, something her mother seemed to set great stock in. Loren's chin had never met her mother's standard. But Loren's chin wasn't the thing that kept her awake at night staring up into nothingness.

The doctor was also very tall. Sitting beneath her, his head was nearly level with hers. She became conscious that he was speaking to her. He was talking about the Indians. She heard him speaking and it seemed somehow to be a foreign tongue. It was as if all the words mixed up with his charming smile and ended up a tangled mess.

For some time now she'd had passing thoughts of death. These thoughts swooped down upon her all unexpected like confused birds and were just as quickly gone.

For just a moment now as the doctor spoke, she felt something blank pressing down upon her. She quickly drew a breath and put a hand to her heart.

"Are you feeling faint?" He looked at her face, his head tilted toward her.

He was much younger than she was, and was simply speaking to her out of charity.

"I'm fine."

Dr. Brown smiled. He had thick side whiskers that moved with his mouth. "Education is practically nonexistent among these tribes. Have you ever considered teaching with a missionary society? Your lovely sister was telling me how your students idolize you. I've heard endless praise. It is someone such as you that I try so very hard to reach on these tours of duty."

She turned her head toward him and stopped thinking of darkness.

"I find it very difficult to speak in front of strangers," he went on, his smile flickering on and off like an electric lamp, "and beg them for money, but I must confess that passion does inspire me. Passion is what is driving in the religious life, I believe, and the teacher must have passion also. Wouldn't you agree, Miss MacGregor?"

Here he stopped and hung his head. "I beg your pardon, I just become so excited when I discuss the cause that when I meet an intelligent woman I can't help but to try to recruit them. Of course you have a life of your own which undoubtedly would take a priority over my mission."

Again, he smiled at her. He had perfectly matched teeth. They seemed to Maybelleen to be made of wax or marble.

"I will be speaking this afternoon of the Lake Mohonk conference and the impact of the Dawes Act on our Indian brethren in the Oklahoma Territory. Oh, that's a place!

"You may in fact have read of our Chicago Presbyterian Missionary Society? *Collier's* did a story on our work just six months ago."

The doctor glanced about the room; the woman wasn't listening and now she was simply staring at him. He began to feel the tiniest bit nervous.

"No children," she suddenly said.

"I beg your pardon?"

"I have no children. I'm not married."

Dr. Brown coughed. "Perhaps you might like a bit more of this fabulous buffet our hostess has put out. I must say I haven't had an ambrosia salad this good in years."

Maybelleen sipped green tea and wished for the sherry hidden in the cedar closet. The sherry took her on long dreamless naps.

"In other words I am not obligated to anything. I can do as I please," she said and wondered what language she was speaking.

"I see," said the doctor.

He noticed that the woman was quite a bit older than he had thought when he'd first seen her across the room. Obviously. Her unusual eyes, shaped like a cat's but black as tar, detracted one's notice at first from the lines at her mouth.

He balanced his teacup on his knee and offered her an almond cookie. Because he had initiated this conversation he didn't know how to end it.

It seemed that the woman was somewhat unbalanced and now that he saw she was at least ten years older than himself, he wished to be gone.

Across the room a group of women were smiling and chatting. Two were quite pretty. One was this woman's sister, her name was Wisteria or Rose or some such climbing plant, and the other one, the blond, was really quite fresh, the way she turned and smiled at him and waved. All the rest were dreary and drab but doubtless had money tucked away in their simple Sunday silks.

This town was not poor. He'd seen that when he'd come in from New Albany across the river. This was one of those little towns that prided itself on its immaculate churches and pristine town square. A town needed money to have pride. Pride was expensive.

Now the blond was beckoning to him to cross the room and join her merry group but he somehow could not think of a way to comfortably extricate himself from this woman who sat in the wing chair like some dispossessed queen. And the silence now was becoming awkward. He hated that.

"I would like that, I think," she said to him then.

She placed the china plate upon the floor with the remaining crab salad left uneaten.

"What?" said the doctor, glancing again about the room.

"To teach those who really need to be taught. I feel I must do something, anything. Have you ever felt that way?"

She lifted from her lap a book upon which she'd rested her tea plate. "Look at this, lying here in my lap, Plato's *Great Dialogues*. How often do you think this book is used for more than a lap table? It was lying here upon this chair when I sat down, as though carefully placed to be read earnestly and often. Yet, I know that it is not. It is here because it has a very pretty red leather cover and looks nice upon the gold fabric. It works with the room, you see, and in my lap also. But I doubt that it has ever been read."

"I see," he said, although he didn't really.

"But you have a calling, as you've named it. You have a cause."

Her eyes caught him then. He felt as though she had touched him, touched his face with her hand, although of course she hadn't. Those hands were now twisting at a green sleeve.

"I would like to know more about this teaching that you propose. I would like to know if it is very far away. But I must tell you I am not interested in missionary work."

"No," said Dr. Brown, "I mean, why?"

"Unlike you, I have absolutely no calling at all. But teach? That I can. That I can do. Not as if it were a calling, not that at all. I mean that it is something that I can do."

He looked again at her face. She faced this appraisal, her expression unchanged.

At first, across the room she'd stood out, being so tall and graceful, and she had beautiful light brown hair, which, from where he'd stood, had seemed charming the way it refused to stay where it belonged. Now, up close, he could see that she was fading.

It occurred to him at that moment that the worst part for this woman was her intelligence, he knew somehow that she was much smarter than he would ever be. This, he saw, would make things hardest of all for her. He'd never thought about a woman in this way before, but with her, he knew that no idle charities would ever be able to occupy her. She was unique somehow, although he didn't know how at all. It made him very uncomfortable. And there was something else about her, something very forward, but somehow disguised. It was a thing she gave off, almost something he could smell.

She breathed out and his face was close, far too close, he realized, and he caught a scent like grass. Like warm, chewed grass. He found himself wondering at that moment what the rest of her might smell like, at the base of her spine, the nape of her neck. She wasn't really that old at all, no, not a spinster yet.

She kept her eyes on his throughout, even as he took in her breath. He suppressed an urge to stroke her hand, caught himself up, and coughed.

"Well, it must be about time," he said. "I see our hostess is shifting us all into the other room. I regret we must interrupt this delightful conversation. Thank you for allowing me to go on."

"When you are done, I will have questions."

"Of course," said the doctor, standing. He smiled down at her and made a small bow.

Ridiculous, he said to himself. This woman was near forty and he was much younger. It was time he got married. No man could be expected to contain himself in the most absurd situations without a wife to sustain him.

"Come," said Eliza Barrymore over a tinkling silver bell, "come take your seats, ladies, you don't know how hard I had to beg to get the good doctor away from those fancy parlors up north." And the hostess came to lead the doctor to the podium in the next room.

"Oh, Eliza," said Ivy in a too-loud voice, "share your cousin with us all. None of us will ever have a chance at such a match, you know." The ladies pretended shock and hid smiles behind their hands.

"Ivy MacGregor!" said the hostess.

The doctor blushed and he never remembered doing that before. He wondered if Maybelleen saw it. But if she did, she gave no indication.

He let the women take his arms and lead him away.

Maybelleen watched them go then lifted the book from

her lap, flipped through it as the sound of chatter began to die down until she came to this part, and read:

> "And can you mention any pursuit of mankind in which the male sex has not all these gifts and qualities in a higher degree than the female? Need I waste time in speaking of the art of weaving, and the management of pancakes and preserves, in which woman-kind does really appear to be great, and in which for her to be beaten by a man is of all things the most absurd?"
>
> "You are quite right in maintaining the general inferiority of the female sex . . ."

Maybelleen closed the book and, standing, placed it upon the seat of the gold chair as it was when she first found it.

Perhaps it did after all, make the perfect decoration.

THE SPEECH

"Ladies," began the newly ordained Dr. Brown.

The little blond had seated herself directly in front of the lectern and her upturned face was fixed raptly upon his. His mother's wifely candidate, cousin Eliza Barrymore, smiled up at him, adoration fixed firmly on her plain face. The silks rustled as the ladies settled.

The doctor watched as Maybelleen MacGregor entered through the parlor doors and sat in the back row.

"There is," said Dr. Brown, "something very great to be said for the generosity of spirit which invites me to be with you today. I will have a very hard time of it competing with Dr. Milton and his well-turned phrases, but I shall do my best to touch your hearts and to perhaps wrest from them the tiniest bit of compassion for a people that, as we sit here now, are living in the most wretched conditions imaginable and need only your help to improve them."

The blond tilted her head to the side and pursed her lips together in a tight smile. Eliza Barrymore clasped her hands and turned to smile at her guests.

"May I beg your indulgence to a speech which I prepared just for your society? It is an untried speech and raw, but I will try to stir your minds and imaginations if I might have your permission."

"Go on, Doctor," said a voice from the audience. "Oh yes, do!" cried another.

Dr. Brown turned his head a moment to the right. His profile was best from that side. He stroked his dark mustache as though truly contemplating how to begin.

"Indians!" he then thundered and banged his hand down upon the lectern. "Wild savages. Crazed killers. Scalping, torture, mindless murder, and gross womanly defilement!"

"Aaaaah," cried out the women. "Ooooh."

"Yes," said the doctor. "This is how we see them. All these things we attribute to the Indian. This is the lurid picture drawn in parlors across this country, painted by magazines and ten-cent novels. Why, for a nickel in St. Louis or Chicago we might see a Wild West show and Indians reprising battles, scalping each fallen American soldier in a mock reenactment of scenes told for our amusement.

"But," said the doctor, pausing once again and looking at his audience, "but . . ."

The ladies leaned toward him. "These are all lies!" Dr. Brown paused and clasped his hands behind his back.

He walked away from the lectern and stood in front of the blond woman in the first row.

"Do you believe that an Indian is a drunkard?" She covered her mouth and giggled. "Do you believe that an Indian is less intelligent or loving than any ordinary man?" The blond shrugged and giggled again.

"There are a people," said Dr. Brown standing in front of the lectern, "that were on this continent long before Christopher Columbus ever dreamed of a ship or uncharted territories. These people lived lives in true Rousseauian fashion, growing old with nature, living and dying purely in tune with the earth until one day, one day, came the white man. Yes, the white men appeared and killed as many of these innocents as they could, divided those they could not, starved them and despised them and then: left them all to slowly die."

Dr. Brown scanned his audience. He stretched out his arms and pulled them in. Quietly then he continued.

"I am a man of God. This I discovered on my first trip out West as a student of theology. There I discovered my duty to bring all people, most especially these children, to His table.

"Now my friends I must tell you that I left a very comfortable life in Chicago, yes, a comfortable life in which I did better than most.

"Ladies, I will confess that I drank a bit, took the name of the Lord our God in vain and yes, I even gambled. I was not a particularly bad man but I was not a good man either. I had no direction in life. None that is until I went West.

"You see, one day a friend took me to attend a conference which has changed my very life. It is true that by then I had already become a minister by choosing God over my petty indulgences. But I awoke to my true responsibility to God and mankind by working on a solution to this problem with the Indians. This, I believe, is God's work for me here. This is my mission."

Dr. Brown stopped and took a sip of water. The ladies turned one to the other, silently communicating their approval of this handsome and so serious young man. Eliza Barrymore patted Ivy MacGregor's hand.

"I will tell you now," said the doctor, "of some of the things I have seen and hope that you might yourselves be moved in some small part. Because if I do not share with others I am not working in God's plan. Here then is a story.

"Now a little over a year ago I was in Indian Territory. I had been assigned to a mission there by the Society and I was trying very hard to learn humbly how to proceed with God's plan for me.

"Well, one day, I left the mission and went alone to take some Bibles and preserved foods to a small band of Kickapoos who were living hand-to-mouth there, right outside of town.

"As I was walking through this settlement of fallen shacks and ragtag lean-tos, an old woman caught my eye. She was leaning against a hut made of sticks and dirty blankets and appeared to be nearly at death's door. But, I must tell you, her face was of such a noble cast, nearly heroic, that I found myself comparing it in that instant to an ancient seeress of Greece and I went to sit beside her.

"I then asked her name but she would not reply and thinking she had no English I put forth some phrases in Arapaho which I had learned from an Indian at the mission. Still she would say nothing.

"While speaking with her, I continually had to brush away flies; the filth was indescribable as human waste and rotting food had been left all about to fester.

"This was assigned land, ladies, and this is the allotment given to this small band. They did not wish to live this way, but they were given no option or alternative.

"Also, I saw no children in the settlement and this concerned me, as one of my duties was to bring the children to our mission school and Bible classes.

" 'Where are the children,' I asked the woman. She turned her face to me and said in English, 'They are dead of the spotted fever.'

" 'Why you speak perfect English!' I said. I was amazed at the clarity of her speech, for it has been wrongly put forth that these people are unable to properly speak.

" 'I speak,' she said, 'but your language is ugly. The children are dead but it is better that they are dead than dragged by you to one of your prison schools.'

" 'Dear woman,' I replied, agitated as you may imagine by her gross misrepresentation, 'our schools are not prisons, they are gifts that we give your children so that they might become something great. And there they learn of God and may then go to heaven.'

"She turned her head away from me.

"She was so very frail and thin and I offered her some of the bread that I had. She refused it, waving her hand at me.

" 'Why won't you eat?' I asked her. Her answer was simple; she wished to die.

"Yes my friends, she was sitting in front of her home waiting for death and she was literally killing herself by starvation.

"Can you imagine this? Can you imagine the horror? I spoke with her then. I spoke with her and said, 'But you cannot make the decision to die. Only God may determine that for you.'

"Then this woman spat upon me. I flinched at first, but remembering the suffering of our Lord, I again tried to reach out to her. But, she did not care, she told me, 'for Christ and his Marys, or any of God's will or purpose.' She had been a Christian, she said, but all that the white man's God had done had been to take her family, take all of her people and kill them all.

" 'Your God,' she told me, 'is the white God and he does not love me.'

"She spat again, this time on the ground, and then she fell back, exhausted, it seemed, from the very effort of speaking at all.

"Well, I could not leave her, seeing that she was close to death and alone. My single purpose then, I determined, was to bring this woman to God before she passed away.

"I sat with her through the evening, we watched together as the sun set and I placed in her hand a Bible.

" 'Please,' I begged her, 'please accept God's love and you will go to a most beautiful heaven.'

"The woman looked at me and said, 'There is no heaven for my people. You have taken heaven away.' She looked at me then very strangely—I will never forget her face—and said, 'You think I cannot die?'

"I begged her to accept Christ but she would not, she

made a strange sign at me with her hands and screamed a long, loud, crazed wail. Then she slumped against the shack and was dead.

"This poor, ignorant woman died in the embrace of evil and ignorance all because of the way the Indian has been previously treated by us, the white conqueror.

"Well, as you must imagine, I cried bitterly for some time, sitting next to this dead woman. I despised myself for my weakness, my inability to reach her before she died.

"I then roused myself and walked about the settlement and attempted to find someone who would bury her at least, but no one would speak to me and at last I returned to bury her alone.

"As I was walking back, a group of men rode into the settlement on horseback.

"When they saw me, I raised up my hands and asked what they wanted. They told me they had come to take an Indian man back to town for stealing. 'We're going to string him up,' the man told me, 'these Indians have got to learn.'

"To the man who appeared their leader I inquired just what it was that the Indian man had stolen.

" 'A mirror,' the man replied, 'and a case of whiskey.'

"The men then proceeded to stomp through the settlement, firing off their guns at will until at last they pulled a poor, dazed man from a shack. Howling, they pitched him upon a horse, bound his hands behind his back, and as they were preparing to ride away, I again accosted them by standing in front of the leader's horse.

" 'You can't hang a man for stealing a mirror and some drink,' I told them.

"The leader laughed at me, and lashed at me with his whip. 'We can, Preacher, and we will.' He promptly then, to impress me, I imagine, wrapped his whip about the poor Indian's neck and dragged him along behind his horse to the edge of the settlement. There they left him.

"No Indian came to the poor man's aid, and I alone ran to his side. Choking and coughing was this poor Indian but this one, this one, ladies, I did manage to save.

"Yes, I took him back with me to the mission and he is now as fine a Christian as you might ever see. We have named him John and he has also become the finest of cooks.

"So this, ladies, is your real Wild West. This is it."

The doctor paused. The women stared up at him.

"I tell you this story to illustrate our ignorance of the plight of these people. They deserve the same treatment that we extend to all the poor and displaced.

"Is an orphan more dear because it is white? I know that I stand on Kentucky soil, ladies. Some of you may whisper among yourselves later saying, 'He's a Northerner, he doesn't understand.' Yet, this is what I know of women. You, with your finer sensibilities, your humble grace, your gentle loving spirit, are the glue of the human race. I know not one of you could deny the tears of a child, whatever color that child may be.

"Men, on the other hand, are made of cruder stuff. Men make war and look upon a child of a different race and say, 'He'll grow up and make war on me. I must destroy him.'

"Women see only the tears of an innocent. Women see only the need for food and sheltering arms. Women understand a child must be clothed and bathed and loved and educated to grow in God's light."

In the audience the women nodded their heads.

"Now, in 1887, President Cleveland signed into law an act that forever changed our Indians' lives. This law is the Dawes Allotment Act, named for that great senator from Massachusetts, who has been a guiding light at the conferences at Mohonk Lake in New York. This law at last gave us a chance to change the Indians' lives.

"We, who are so fortunate, have been given a way to humanize the Indian so that we may all live in harmony, so that the Indian might grow to love these United States as fervently as do we all.

"Now, I won't bore you with politics but will tell you simply that what the Dawes Act has done is to give the Indian the right to own the land beneath his feet and to abolish forever the inhumane reservation system that segregates one Indian from another and creates these tribes of people who cannot function among us as individuals.

"Now you may have read about our new Oklahoma Territory, probably heard some horror stories about Indians thrown off their land.

"It simply isn't true. No, what's been done has been to encourage the Indian to make his own way.

"We must understand fully the significance of this. You see, by owning his own land, the Indian becomes his own master. He learns the joy of tilling his own ground and the rewards of his labors. This is the key to bringing the Indian into our stream of life, this is the true Americanization of the Wild West.

"For as the Indian departs from his tribal system, he embraces his new, independent life. He sends his children to school, he attends church, and gradually grows into a true and fine American citizen. It is our duty to bring him to us and embrace him.

"Ladies, here we are, reeling as our new century opens. As a nation we have marched steadfastly toward progress. All women are equal as will soon be proven by the power they will wield with the vote. And yes, I am a fervent supporter of the Movement. But we must ask ourselves if we wish to be truly an advanced civilization, why are there still a people in this great land who are held outside? Even the colored folk are treated better than our Indian brethren.

"With the passage of the Dawes Act, First Presbyterian Missionary Society of Greater Chicago sent forth its ministers to help the Indian adapt to his new environment.

"We provide schools for their children, churches for their beginning communities, and aid with their farms, even to driving the mules ourselves. And in just a few years our progress has been enormous.

"In Texas and Arizona alone, we have brought forth five new little towns peopled with Indians who do not live on reservations, who send their children to us for education, and who have been taught to reject their tribal system in exchange for belonging to the greatest tribe of all: the American.

"The town in which I work is in the new Oklahoma Territory. Dear ladies, in that town there is a little boy named Tomas. His father is dead and his mother works hard at trying to farm but she has little success because she can't afford even the cost of a plow. But, with great fortitude and struggle, Tomas has learned Latin. We study sometimes late into the night by candlelight.

"Now, my friends, Tomas would like to be a doctor when he grows up but it is very unlikely that will ever happen because there is no money for education.

"What will become of Tomas? Or his mother? Will they become tired of striving and run back to the reservation?

"No! We cannot permit this! It is only with your help, ladies, that this work can be done because the cost is enormous. Without you ladies, Tomas will most likely become discouraged and eventually perhaps even turn to alcohol when he has nothing else to turn to. You see the current government doesn't fully understand why we need to take these Indians off their reservations and educate them apart.

"But without help, my mission is only an empty hand."

Dr. Brown stopped. He turned his head to the ceiling and said, "Please help me on my mission."

"Oh," said a woman, "I'll help. Shall we pass a hat?"

"Thank you," said the doctor, "but we need no hat. Instead, if you wish to place your donation, whatever you believe you might contribute, in this glass bowl on the table which has kindly been provided by our hostess."

The doctor beamed. The rest was easy. He had not yet been appointed a congregation but he had the greatest certainty that he would make an enormous contribution. Why, by forty who knew where it might all lead.

He stepped away from the podium wrapped up warm and glowing in the blanket of his humming words.

As the women approached him, each pausing to drop into the Waterford bowl several notes, he forgot for a moment just how fine were his blue eyes, how select his fingers and how singular his profile. For he was good. And the story about the old woman and the mythical Tomas? Why, God would excuse him for elaborating on something that only half happened because of the good the story had done.

Just look! The bowl was now crammed full of money for his beloved Indians. It was very nearly loaves and fishes, this conversion of his few words to many mighty dollars.

He dimpled beneath his muttonchop whiskers as women reached out to shake his hand.

But then that woman was there.

She stood behind the crowd, her height, her bright colors overpowering the rest. And the little blond, close now, had a distinct mustache and was sweating beneath the arms of her tight gray suit.

"Yes," he replied to some question that he half heard. "Of course," to his cousin's request that he join them for a light dessert.

She simply stared at him from the back of the room.

"Miss MacGregor," he said, and all the ladies turned their heads in a perfect choreography. "Miss MacGregor, have you a question?" His voice sounded hoarse and hollow in his ears.

Maybelleen tucked her hair back from her face and looked directly at the doctor. "I have many questions, I suppose. One might be what the Indians, whom you refer to as 'ours' and 'yours,' think about what you refer to as 'humanizing' them, but I think that I should like to ask that of them in person. Another question would be, when might I expect to join your community in the West?"

"What?" said Dr. Brown. He smiled at the ladies surrounding him, but their backs were turned away from him. They were all staring at Maybelleen MacGregor.

"Why that's a great question, indeed. We must ask ourselves if we are in a position to make such a commitment, if this is valid, if this is motivated"—he cleared his throat—"by, um, God."

"Nonsense," replied Maybelleen. "On the God matter, I mean. I am motivated by a true desire to do something meaningful with my life before I die and I am a certified and qualified teacher. Will you have me?"

"May!" cried Ivy. "Whatever are you going on about? I don't think you're at all well, honey." Ivy moved to join her sister.

"I am qualified or I am not."

"Maybelleen MacGregor you've gone completely mad!" Opal Dillon, of the fair hair and mustache—actually a MacGregor first cousin—took Maybelleen's hand.

"Cousin Opal, I think I know what I'm talking about. Excuse me." She pulled her hand from the other woman's. "I don't see what's mad about trying to do something with your life."

"Maybelleen, you'll shock Mama to death!"

"Close your mouth Ivy and stop gasping like that. You look like a fish. Opal, please stop pawing at me.

"For the first time in my life I feel like I'm finally making sense. Ivy, I will walk a bit, the air in here is too close. Please pick me up as you drive out. I'll be on the road. As to Mama, you can drag her to your pretty little house and good luck trying. And Dr. Brown, consider this an earnest application. I will expect your answer by tomorrow. I will, of course, need to make a few arrangements."

"Walking in your good shoes?" screeched Ivy.

Maybelleen wrapped herself in her paisley shawl and walked out of the parlor. The ladies heard her tight hard step on the oak entry floor then the door closed and she was gone.

"She's not well. She doesn't really mean it," said her sister to the assemblage.

The women began to circle about, whispering and nearly colliding until their hostess clapped her hands.

"Now then," she said, "let us have some punch and cookies. Mrs. Tarryton's cook has baked us some of her famous lemon bars."

"Perhaps you should go after your sister," said Eliza Barrymore to Ivy MacGregor.

"But that's just it, Eliza! She knows I can't drive that horse!"

"Well then, sit down and we'll think of something. Here. Have a lemon bar. Perhaps she simply needs to cool her head. If Loren Simpson would propose to her this never would happen at all. Women need a man to keep their wits about them."

Ivy ate four or five of the pastries and felt distinctly ill. Indians of all things! She now knew for certain that her older sister was just like their mother. My God, she thought as she forced herself to eat another lemon bar—they were very good—I hope it's not hereditary. What would Sam think?

Dr. Brown switched the big white horse. Maybelleen's sister kept on and on, "Oh where is she? What is wrong with her? Dr. Brown, do you think she is serious?"

The doctor kept looking ahead for the woman who somehow drew him on and on down this little dirt road to who knew where.

"There she is!" screamed Ivy, half standing and pointing to a figure on the side of the road nearly a half mile away.

"Please sit, Miss MacGregor, I think you're disturbing this horse."

A horrid old beast, thought the doctor. He'd rarely seen such an obstinate animal in his life.

"Oh Milk doesn't mind if Maybelleen's near. Milk loves her, he does, don't you honey?"

Ivy leaned toward the horse and it pulled off to the side of the road, baring its teeth. "He bites, but May loves him and won't have another. Oh Doctor, don't let her teach any Indians, she doesn't know a thing about any old Indians. She must stay here with us. She's not been too well you see lately, but I feel and Sam feels that she just needs to come and live with us and have a full and happy life and she'd thought she'd marry Loren but he's just as stubborn as this horse and . . . oh! No! It's not her at all!"

It was now obvious that what they'd thought was Maybelleen was a piece of billowing green fabric caught on a barbed-wire fence.

"What is that?" said Ivy. The doctor said nothing.

It was getting late and they hadn't discussed how he would ever get back to town from their farm, wherever that was. Maybelleen obviously knew where she lived and could walk perfectly well. There was no need for concern.

But still, as the sun began to fall, he found himself scanning the roadside woods for a sign of her among the trees.

Finally they found her, kid boots in hand, twirling a large stick, and it seemed as they came upon her that she was singing.

Hello was all she'd said as she'd climbed into the trap. She'd taken the reins from the doctor and the awful horse had tossed its head and lifted its legs in a pretty trot. They came to the farm in no time at all.

In the reddish light of the setting sun the farmhouse appeared around a bend in the road. It was three stories and square, painted white, with a large front porch. The windows reflected the ruby-red light of the sun. The doctor could see a large green barn and acres of pasture spreading out to the east. At the back of the house, a dark woods hovered.

"Who tends to the farm?" he asked.

"Oh, we have people," said Ivy, "since Daddy died, we've always had the same people. "Sometimes Mama gets upset about it because it was her family's farm and she thinks we should all get up at dawn and take care of things like she used to do. She just won't accept that ladies don't do that. Why, just a week ago we found her wandering over there among the cornstalks. We have to watch her careful now, you know. Last fall she killed a bull by herself because she said it wouldn't breed good stock . . . oh, well, never mind. Mama's just old. You know how old folks get."

"Of course," said Dr. Brown. Maybelleen laughed.

The doctor saw no one at all, no sign of life as they pulled up the gravel drive. There was not a light on anywhere in the house and no one came out to take the buggy. Maybelleen dropped them off under the portico. He stood there for a moment watching her drive away, the gravel crushing under the wheels, until the trap disappeared behind the house.

The mother joined them for dinner. Ivy kept up a constant happy chatter and Maybelleen tapped at her water glass with a spoon, not eating or speaking at all. She stared at all around almost as though she wasn't quite sure where she was.

"Preacher," said the mother, "where do you preach?"

"Out West," he answered.

The food was excellent and served by a tiny Irish girl who blended into the shadows of the oil lamp.

"I don't usually see many people," the mother had told

him. "My husband liked to have folks about but now he's dead and I have things the way I like 'em. I ain't been well, my rheumatism been acting up. But it's good having a preacher man to supper. Good luck. You married?"

"Mama!" said Ivy.

"Hush your mouth little girl," said the mother, "you got you a man."

"No ma'am I'm not married." The doctor nodded at the little serving girl when she offered him another slice of the rare tenderloin beef.

"Mama, he's practically engaged to Eliza Barrymore!"

"Well," said the doctor, "that's not exactly right, I mean, my mother, well, you see, I'm not . . ."

"You ain't made up your mind then," said the old woman. She grinned with a full mouth of mashed potatoes.

The doctor wondered at this woman. She certainly didn't seem to fit into this elegant room.

"Maybelleen did it," she said. "You were lookin' around. It was May. Got good taste, ain't she? But she's educated. Still, no one'll take her. She's a little old see, but she's a smart one. Still can have chillun too. Why, I had this one"—and she pinched Ivy's hand—"when I was forty and four. Pretty, ain't she? But dumb as can be."

"Oh, Mama." Ivy coughed into her napkin and stood up.

"Sit down! What's wrong with the truth, honey? You know you ain't good with that reading and all.

"They say I'm crazy now, Preacher, 'cause I say what I want. As I'm fond of sayin', I might find Hell just walking down a dark hallway but then, I ain't particularly lookin' for heaven. I've no use for white or plunkin' on harps, if you know what I mean.

"Now these two girls of mine—I had a boy, too, but he drowned when he was ten, he was the best of them all, but what can you do? These girls of mine has had educations. Yes. Educations at a fancy school in Louisville.

"This one, this here, is a teacher. And this one, the pretty one, she can write more'n her name. She's marryin' a doctor. My husband, see, became a wealthy man from plantin' tobacky and he could read and write. He sent these here girls to school. May went to college. That's right. Teacher's school. Sharp as a tack. May, read him something."

"No, Mama."

"I see," said the doctor. He'd never had radishes in mint gravy before. They melted on the tongue. He looked at May-belleen in the lamplight and she looked very soft and round. If only she wouldn't smile that way, out of focus. It was rude. It was excluding. Selfish, he found himself thinking. Keeping everything to herself, like a cat with its cream.

"Now my May is smart as all git out and she knows all about religion and such. I mean fancy religion, like yours more'n likely. She was always wantin' to go off to Europe and see churches and whatnot. I think she's fond of that popery and all and she'd make a damn fine wife for any preacher."

"Mama, you can't force Maybelleen down everybody's throat!" cried Ivy, turning a pretty pink.

Maybelleen twirled her spoon.

"Ivy Clementine, you can git yourself off to bed now. You're lookin' pinched. Your doctor ain't gonna want a pinched and wasted gal, is he?"

"Doctor Brown, I'm so sorry, she's not well—" began Ivy.

"Go," said her mother. "And Maybelleen, you go sit yourself out on the porch. I'll have Miranda here bring you folks something out there."

Ivy excused herself and with a pout at her mother, said to the serving girl, "Miranda, bring me up some warm milk and cookies."

"Yes, we'll fatten you up," said the mother.

Maybelleen stood and pulled on her shawl.

"My mother hasn't any use for me, Dr. Brown." Maybelleen walked over to her mother and gave her a kiss on the cheek. Her mother batted her away.

"Well, that may be, but perhaps he might."

Maybelleen paused for a moment at a crystal vase on the sideboard, ran her fingers over it, then left the room.

With Maybelleen gone the room seemed somehow smaller to the doctor. He pushed back his plate. The old woman was pointing at him with a silver fork.

"Anyway, Doctor. What, you're a doctor too? Anyway, my girls, and I do love them dearly, don't really have any use for me, you see, because I'm just a plain old farm woman who ain't had no fancy education and don't have no fancy manners.

"You think I know any of their friends? Why no! They always say I'm sick if they go callin'. I embarrass 'em, see. But that's alright. That's alright. My only worry is this farm. You like farmin'? No? Well. Ivy's man likes it fine. Fact is"— and the mother lowered her voice and leaned over to the doctor—"he's just told her that he's movin' to town, fact is, he's takin' over the farm when they're married. So you see, money ain't always the root of evil."

"You mean you bribed him?" asked the doctor. "I mean, excuse me, that must be a great comfort to you."

Dr. Brown felt very warm. He was flushed and could feel perspiration clotting up beneath his spring suit. He had certainly eaten far too much. "I must say I've seldom had such a wonderful meal."

"May can cook," said the mother. "Just like this here dinner."

For some odd reason, perhaps the digesting of the rich gravy, the doctor felt all akimbo, almost as though he'd fallen into a pool of warm water but water in which he could breathe without distress.

He smiled at the dining room, the elegant draperies and the ivy-patterned English wallpaper. "And there is some money for my girl May, too, Mr. Preacher."

In the center of the table, tulips were arranged in a solid silver bowl.

"I beg your pardon?"

"Yes indeed. Whatever good is money for if you don't spend it while you're here? Now you go on out on the porch and I'll send you something with the girl. She's Irish, that one, but I can almost trust her because I raised her myself. She knows something about farmin' that girl does, too bad she's got that blood though. The Irish are never any good."

"I am of Celtic descent." He had no idea at all why he'd said that.

"Ha!" laughed the woman. "With my May it won't matter, she's got the will of seven devils. Now, skeedaddle."

With that the mother waved him away as though he were a lowly courtier. He wiped his mustache and gave her a bow. As he turned to leave she fell to eating with great gusto, the utensils scraping across the plate sounding like aggravated bones.

He passed through a dark front parlor and followed a narrow hallway to a door that stood open to the front porch.

For a moment he paused there in the doorway. He didn't see her sitting on the porch and the spell was beginning to wear. He began to feel foolish and unhappy at being at this remote location, away from the light of the big cities where he knew he shone the brightest. Instead, here he was on a lonely farm with an old lunatic and her unmarried spinster daughter under the light of a very disturbing blue gibbous moon.

"Hello?" he said and the crickets answered. "Hello?"

"I'm here."

He moved toward the voice at the edge of the porch. May-belleen sat upon the step. He could smell lilacs sleeping in the earth. The night was loud and the farm smells disturbing.

"Well, Miss MacGregor, I must say you've a fine place here."

"And you wonder how I could leave it?"

"No. I didn't mean that. I mean, we haven't really spoken much about the pros and cons of this adventure . . ."

"Marriage?"

"I mean the mission work."

"Oh, of course." Maybelleen laughed. "I'm sorry, Doctor, if my mother alarmed you. You needn't worry, I'm not interested in you in that way."

"No? Oh. Of course not. Your mother is really delightful, though, so very . . ."

"Honest? Well. Yes, she is that. You can't cross her though, she tried to stab our farm foreman with pinking shears when he insisted on putting up the hay two weeks later than she believed was time."

"My! Have you never considered that she might be more comfortable somewhere where she has fewer responsibilities?"

"Actually she was right. There was an awful storm that whipped through here, full of hail and ice. It ruined the hay."

"I would say that your leaving here would leave your

mother and your sister at such a loss, leave them so alone, that I don't quite know how they'd get along."

"They'll be fine, Dr. Brown. They always were. I've never done anything that made the slightest difference to either one of them. Oh, they may say I have, a lent blouse here to my little sister, a story told, some laughter for my mother, but that's all. My mother would be no different now if I'd never been born at all. She's a woman of her own devising and I admire her for it.

"Dr. Brown, I have made a decision with my life. It happened when you spoke with me about a mission. Unless you find me wanting in qualifications, I plan on accepting the post you initially proposed to me."

"Pardon?"

"You did. You said something about meeting intelligent ladies, some nonsense or other, and the lack of good teachers. So, I'm a good teacher and I accept."

"I was not quite serious—"

"Then you should not have spoken."

She turned away from him. He stood behind her and momentarily hung his head like a slapped child. Then his teeth clenched.

Maybelleen turned her face to him and it was outlined in window light. "I believe now that there is a certain beauty to directness. I will not ask your pardon and I do not believe in cruelty. Life is short. We all know this but somehow we all become aware of it at different stages. I became aware of it a long time ago.

"Do you know what it's like, Doctor, to get up every day with every intention of doing something and finding absolutely nothing to do? Eventually it wears you down. I think this happens to everyone sooner or later but with me it happened sooner. There are times I look in the mirror and the face I see is completely gray. There's no color at all, as though I didn't even have any blood left. But somehow I know that that's not it. I just didn't know what to do.

"And then I met you. You can ascribe it to God. Well, isn't that the way it's supposed to work? God works miracles and moves in mysterious ways? You then have gained something here, Doctor, some form of convert. And although my faith is only in my own ability to fight back and not give in to that gray face in the mirror, perhaps somewhere down the line I'll fall over on my deathbed and see the light you are constantly beckoning us with."

She moved and the fabric of her skirt rustled. The wind had come up. The doctor began to feel the pounding of his heart. It was so loud in his ears that it completely drowned out the sound of crickets and night things. This blanket of darkness fell on him as it had when he was a child. The same fear of closets and corners and under the bed. It grew colder. It was still just barely spring.

"Do you understand, Dr. Brown? Even if you don't, it doesn't matter. Say that you saved my life."

"Oh, of course I see," he said and he didn't at all. She was mad, she spoke of things that he never thought of, not really. He was a laugher, yes, with a beautiful smile and she, she was old and beginning to fade away into whatever it was that she had described. But he did very much, right then, wish to kiss her. So, when she rose from the stair, right below him, he reached for her and then he was pulling her to him and her hair smelled of lilacs and earth and bones and blue moonlight.

He felt her lips open and he pushed in his tongue. He pulled her to him harder, saying, "Dear, my dear."

She laughed. He turned around.

The maid was standing behind them, a tray in her hand.

"Your mama sent you sherry and the genleman some port."

"Thank you, Miranda," Maybelleen said.

The doctor took the glass from the tray.

"When do we leave?" she said, her eyes on his. She smiled. It was the smile that did him in. She beamed it directly at him, hiding nothing.

"Leave?" His heart pounded on, on and on.

"For the Wild West," said Maybelleen.

Afterward he often wondered if the old woman had somehow put a country spell on him, or drugged his water glass at dinner, for he answered the woman before him with, "In a week, after my speech in Louisville." It seemed then, with those crazy night sounds coming at him from all around, completely natural.

"Shall I come with you?"

"To Louisville? Well, after all it might be best." The port was changed and sour and he threw it into the bushes. "It might be a good idea for you to get a general understanding of the Mission."

"I see you didn't care for the port; ask Miranda for some of the bourbon. My father kept some wonderful bourbon."

And she went into the house.

In the strange, soft bed he listened to the floors creak and sigh. He couldn't sleep and left the next morning on a borrowed sorrel mare to explain to his cousin that he couldn't be expected to be mixed and matched like sofa fabric.

He had found another bride.

Margaret

Behind and Ahead

My grandmother always said she was grateful. She wasn't grateful to any particular God, I don't think. I don't believe she thought much about religion. My grandparents never went to church and me and Malcolm never went either.

The first time I was in a church was when I attended a wedding when I was fifteen. It had never occurred to me that it was odd that I never saw a Bible around the house until I was around ten or eleven and began to be jealous of friends who seemed to have some sort of pipeline to God by virtue of their attendance at church and Sunday school.

I didn't know why my grandparents never went to any of the local churches. I realize now how strange that was. They were isolated from the community, that much I do know. I don't recall them having any friends, only relatives. Now, Aunt Opal has explained to me that my grandmother stepped away from the community when she stood up for her sister, when the whole world condemned Maybelleen, Grandmother Ivy told them all to go to hell. When Malcolm and me were little that was already long past, but I guess people remembered that there was something about the Dyes, something they weren't supposed to like about them. Because people always stayed away. We never attended socials. I never ate watermelon at a Sunday-school picnic.

But still Grandmother used to say, "I'm grateful."

She inherited my brother Malcolm and me. She was grateful that she had us even though to get us she'd lost her only child, our mother.

We don't remember Dad and Mother. Malcolm and me spent hours when we were little looking at photographs of these people who produced us without ever feeling like we came from them at all.

Our parents died crossing a bridge in a storm in 1928. The bridge collapsed into the Ohio River. They were on their way back from Chicago. Dad sold insurance and they'd driven to Chicago for a conference. It was the first time they'd ever gone on a big trip together.

That's all we really know. What my mother thought about, I have no idea. I laid awake sometimes and wondered what must have gone through their minds at the moment that bridge fell apart. They were young and in love and I used to speculate on whether they held each other in those last moments, if they clung together as the car slid down into the ice water of the river. And, since they never found the bodies, if they had floated out an underwater car window, wrapped in each other's arms. In my mind they were always young and wrapped in each other's arms. Never did I find a hint of myself. It was always just them twined together.

So we were our grandparents' children. That's how we were raised.

We didn't spend nights sobbing into our pillows and moaning about our orphan status. We never felt like orphans.

Grandpa was a doctor but he gave up medicine for farming. The farm meant everything. Malcolm and me grew up eating carrots pulled right out of the dirt and wiped clean on wet grass. I never had a canned vegetable until I moved away.

Grandpa was a good farmer. He managed well and we were prosperous. We had more than twelve hundred acres producing corn, soybeans, alfalfa, and of course, the king crop, tobacco.

When we were small we had dairy cows but Grandpa gave them up for beef cattle. I was always sad about that. The dairy cows were gentle and had enormous liquid eyes with long eyelashes. The Black Angus were belligerent and stupid. They were only good for steak. The bull was always chasing me when we had to cross the field where they grazed.

And we had to cross that field to get to the cemetery.

I was eight years old when I discovered Maybelleen. I found her in the graveyard. After seeing that lonesome marker I went home and said to my grandmother, "Who was Maybelleen?"

She hadn't looked at me but answered the wall instead. "My sister."

"She's dead?"

I remember Grandma was making an angel food cake, fluffing the egg whites, beating them 'round and 'round, the whisk in the blue stoneware bowl was spinning the eggs, coaxing them to peak.

"How'd she die?"

Grandma had stopped beating the whites and sat down on a chair. "Oh," she said, "she got killed." And when she looked out the window, there were tears in her eyes. The only other time she cried was when she talked about Regina, my mother.

But I was merciless. "How was she killed?" I could smell something here and I had to know. Even at eight I knew that grave in the cemetery was different than the others.

"How?"

"She was hanged, Margaret. Now that's enough."

She stood up and dabbed at her eyes with her apron and turned her back to me.

But of course I danced around her—this was miraculous—saying, "Hanged? Hanged? Who hung her, Grandma? Why'd they hang her? Who did it?"

"I won't talk about it anymore now, Margaret. Oh, now look! My eggs have fallen."

And she wouldn't talk about it.

But my great-aunt was hanged! And put up in a corner of the cemetery and my grandmother wouldn't talk about it. Now my life had begun, I felt. Now this was something that stirred in me and woke me up.

I found the photo drawer in the bottom of my grandpa's bureau.

In the photo drawer were several old photographs of people I'll never know; men with handlebar mustaches who stared at the lens with the intensity of prophets and women in lovely dresses long since gone to the moths.

But there was a woman in one of the photographs that I would stare at for hours. Her slanting dark eyes gave her an exotic look, almost Chinese. The photograph was a portrait taken in 1898. The name and date were written on the back in a slurred hand in green India ink. Maybelleen.

There was nothing in that picture to let me know she'd soon hang. It was a woman from another time. A woman in a high-necked white blouse with hair escaping around her ears and a fringed shawl that seemed on the verge of slipping away.

Gradually, I wore Grandmother Ivy down. She told me more about Maybelleen, how she'd left home to teach the Indians out West with a preacher from Chicago. The preacher had been somehow promised to another woman, it was confusing, said Grandmother, what exactly was what. But when he left with Maybelleen it caused a scandal, although, she said, Maybelleen did nothing wrong, it was the other woman. The other woman claimed the preacher had proposed to her and had published in the newspaper a declaration to sue for breach of promise. It was, said Grandmother, "very ugly and not worth talking about."

"She stole the preacher, then?" I'd asked, wondering how such a thing could be done. It seemed to me, with my limited background, that snatching a preacher was akin to stealing a prayer halfway through the atmosphere.

"The better woman won," Grandma Ivy said then, her eyes all gone wildfire. "Eliza Barrymore was always a liar, the witch."

"Who's Eliza Barrymore?" I'd asked, knowing I'd hit something raw.

"Dead."

That's all she'd say on that subject.

But then, Grandmother told me, something happened out

West, something that caused Maybelleen to lose her mind. In her confused state—for Grandma Ivy said she'd always been of a fragile mind, "she was smarter than wise" was exactly what Grandma said—she'd taken up with a man with a bad reputation. An outlaw. A man who had a gang and robbed trains and banks.

And Maybelleen had lost her mind.

That's what Grandma Ivy said. It just wasn't her fault.

That was how, said Grandmother, she'd ended up the way she had, because of this man with the bad reputation.

But is that any reason to hang someone?

"He was an outlaw," my grandmother had said, her voice hushed as though someone might hear.

Oh. And was she an outlaw too?

"They say she was," said my grandmother, "but I never believed what they said. She was my sister and a good woman, although no one ever wants to believe it. She just went off and lost her mind."

Did she love him?

"Humpf!" said Grandma Ivy. "Love! Maybelleen couldn't have loved a bad man. He bewitched her, hypnotized her. She was always dreaming and that left her weak and open to such things. Love! No, she took after our mama. She was troubled in the mind."

"Troubled how?" For this touched something in me even then.

"Not right. Never mind, Margaret. Enough." And she'd send me out to pull radishes, or cut lettuce for dinner.

And that was the story of Maybelleen. Grandmother would never tell more. Just went off and lost her mind. Like taking a bus to Lexington and leaving your mind behind with a package on the seat.

From that time on, I told Maybelleen everything.

I went to visit Maybelleen under the stars, the moon, and the rain until I grew up and moved away. I told her everything, because being an outlaw, I always figured she'd understand.

Eventually of course, I found out more. There were newspaper articles and books, and of course, that movie, supposedly based on Maybelleen's life.

My great-aunt had been a celebrity of sorts; she was the second and last woman executed by hanging in the state of Texas. The first, Chipita Rodriguez, was hanged on Friday the thirteenth in 1863 for allegedly stabbing a man and leaving him dead in the creek behind her house.

There appears to never have been any direct evidence linking Chipita to the dead man. But they hanged her anyway. I figure she managed to make herself pretty unpopular. Women killed any number of men out West and never got hanged for it.

Chipita's ghost still haunts that creek, they say, and no one will build on the land. Not even cattle will graze down by the creek where she is supposed to walk in the early evening, trailing a hangman's rope behind her.

Maybelleen shot at people, though it was never proven that she actually killed anyone. It seems her greatest crime, in the eyes of the jury, was loving a man who'd killed quite a few. Like Chipita Rodriguez, Maybelleen MacGregor was never successfully linked to anyone's murder. But the jury, comprised of twelve men—one of whom it later turned out, was wanted in Montana for stealing cattle and hanged himself—found her guilty.

My great-aunt Maybelleen was hanged on November 23, 1902. She was charged with the murder of Little Red O'Brien. A Texas Ranger.

She said she didn't do it but she wouldn't say who did.

And no one was interested in the fact that money she'd stolen with Bill was given to Indians. I think that made them only want to hang her more.

OUTLAWS ON MURDER SPREE
Oklahomans Have Had Enough
by Johnathan C. Bride, Editor

Last Sunday in a spectacular blaze of gunfire, the outlaw known as Mexican Bill and his paramour, Maybelleen, along with their wild gang of robbers held up a saloon in our town of Guthrie.

The robbery took place at approximately 2:00 P.M. when most citizens were at church services. Those in the tavern (primarily cowhands and day workers) were playing checkers and cards and were completely unaware that the group of outlaws was among them.

Seymour Gunther, an eyewitness and son of Reverend Elijah Gunther, gave the following account.

Mr. Gunther, who happened to be delivering firewood and was not among those consuming alcohol, told this reporter that a woman of approximately thirty to thirty-four years old approached the barkeeper and asked for a glass of soda water. The barkeeper complied and when he had served her, she removed a Smith & Wesson .32-caliber pistol from her handbag and demanded that he place all monies in her open handbag. It was at that moment that Mr. Gunther and the other customers noticed that four men had placed themselves strategically in the tavern and had guns trained on all around.

The barkeep, Lowell Peerce, complied by placing all bills and coins in the bag. It was at this moment that our witness, Mr. Gunther, noticed that although the men were masked, one man had waist-length black hair. It was in this way that he identified the robber, Mexican Bill.

As the group prepared to depart the tavern, Mr. Peerce in a vain attempt to halt the robbery, took a Winchester Carbine from behind the bar. His heroic effort was thwarted when the outlaw called Mexican Bill noted his action and fired two shots, killing Mr.

Peerce outright. The outlaws then began firing over the heads of the terrified customers, who by this time were arrayed beneath the tables in the tavern.

As this reporter has pointed out in past editorials, taverns have no business serving alcohol on Sundays. Although it has been argued that these saloons have a justified presence in our towns, it is not too much to demand that the citizenry might enjoy one day of peace per week.

The amount of noise, hollering, and gunfire that arises from these establishments have pushed law-abiding citizens to the limit.

It might also be pointed out that the sheriff of Guthrie, Mr. Daniel O'Callahan, is up for reelection on Thursday of next week and if Guthrie's citizens are tired of not being able to walk around in their own town on a Sunday afternoon without a bloodbath, a vote given to his opponent, Reverend Gunther, who held the former post of Sheriff in Golden, Utah, might give honest citizens a respite from Sunday horrors. Reverend Gunther is wholly opposed to serving alcohol on the Sabbath and is the organizer of the Anti-Saloon League.

Following is a description of the outlaw band: Mexican Bill is approximately thirty-two years old, stands six feet tall, and is said to be a deadly shot. He has waist-length black hair and is of Indian or Mexican descent. His lover, Maybelleen MacGregor, is a former schoolteacher. She is thirty-eight years old, white, has light brown hair and is considered extremely dangerous. Another of the gang is Stuart Ray Colvin, known as "Mad Pup." He is easily identified by his youth. He also has dimples on both cheeks. The other two are unidentified. One is a negro of approximately fifty years of age and the last has a clubfoot, also fifty or so.

Although a posse was formed, none of the outlaws were discovered and it is assumed that they have a hideout somewhere in Indian Territory. A bounty of $1,000 has been offered by the United States Texas Rangers for the live capture of Mexican Bill or Maybelleen MacGregor.

This reporter urges the death penalty for these criminals. The West has been won by hard work and honesty and these villainous types must be taught a lesson at the end of a rope. It also might be noted that if the saloon had not been open, this hideous scene would never have occurred. "Ye shall reap as ye sow"!

I found that article folded up in the bottom of my grandfather's bookcase in his office. He'd marked it in pencil, "Old newspaper from Guthrie, Oklahoma. Regarding Maybelleen. Save."

After that, I found out all I could. When Grandpa had to go into Louisville on business, he'd give me money for a movie and I'd go to the library and read and read.

I found out that the newspapers had swarmed in from as far away as New York to see it; a woman who'd defied the law, hanged by the neck.

They say there was a crowd of more than five hundred waiting for her when she was taken out of the jail at 11:50 in the morning.

At first, say the papers, almost all the women were hooting and shaking their fists. One reporter said, "I have never seen such hatred in the faces of honest women. You almost had to wonder; what is it they are afraid of?"

They took her up the stairs of the new-built scaffold, placed a black cotton bag over her head.

Were children watching? No one ever mentioned that.

She never cried, she held up her head to them all. The crowd, which had been shouting "Whore" and "Sinner," quieted down when she stood up there on the scaffold and looked out at them all. The sheriff stood to one side and a preacher on the other. She said to them, "If you need me to die, then I'll do it as gracefully as I can. I only hope you'll get something from it."

The preacher then asked her if she would beg God's forgiveness. "God isn't judging me," she'd said. "You are."

"Will you accept God's love?" he asked her then.

"I'm going straight into love. That's why I'm dying. Even if I only go to dust then it'll be the same dust as Bill's."

Then the sheriff, because that's who had to actually perform the execution, put the black bag over her head. The papers said he whispered something to her as he did it. They say she smiled at him before that awful thing was drawn down over her face.

A Kansas paper said it was deathly quiet, not a sound to be heard.

"The air itself held its breath when at high noon they dropped her through the trapdoor. Many in the crowd turned away."

But she didn't die. That was the horrible thing. Several women fainted to see her twisting at the end of the rope. She jumped and danced until a single shot was fired. A bullet struck her through the right breast.

Then she died.

"There was none of the usual revelry associated with gatherings of this sort when Maybelleen MacGregor finally met her Maker. Instead, there were the sounds of sobbing from the crowd and hardened men were seen to wipe away tears. No one apparently minded that the outlaw was shot through the heart by someone unknown in the crowd. You could almost say a sigh of relief was to be heard. This reporter is compelled to go on the record stating that such barbarity as public executions should be left behind with the Romans," wrote Simon Wintereason of the *Sandy River Gazette*.

After Maybelleen was dead, something strange happened. The wind began to blow incredibly hard and the sky grew so dark that it seemed like night.

Here is what another reporter wrote when it was over:

"A great wind came up, as though the Almighty himself had something to say about the whole affair, as though the One above us was moved to comment." This was from the *Boulder Mountaineer*, reported by Charles Chase.

Because right then the wind began to howl and everything was blowing this way and that. The wind caused the church bell to start ringing and the timber of the scaffold began to creak so loud it seemed to scream like a woman. Dozens of hats flew from ladies' heads, horses went wild, and then someone was heard to shout "Twister!" and everyone began to scatter through the streets.

The scaffold where Maybelleen was still hanging twisted and turned. One woman said she looked back and saw the timber form itself right into a cross with Maybelleen swinging at its middle.

A few minutes later a tornado roared through the east side of town. The winds pulled up the scaffold and Maybelleen too, ripped up the sidewalk boards and sprayed nails into the air. People were danced about like toys and two were killed by flying timber. They say a horse went flying through the air like Pegasus and was never found again.

The walls of the jail were thrown up into the air and landed on Main Street in a pile of rubble. Maybelleen's body was snatched up and flown onto the roof of the church. They say the scaffold was blown to bits and the sheriff was killed when the cross beam smacked him on the head.

The reporters had a field day when they got back home. They tied in Maybelleen's story to the destruction of Sodom and Gomorrah.

And, they never hanged another woman in Texas.

But I always wondered who fired that shot. No one ever knew for sure. Some say it was the one called Young Pup, because they never got him, you know. But no one ever knew. Whoever it was got away in the storm.

Nobody wrote much about her after that. If was as if everybody just wanted to forget.

Then in 1948, after the war, a writer from Hollywood had written a letter to my grandmother, asking if he could interview her for a script he wanted to write about Maybelleen.

My grandmother refused but that horrible movie came out anyway.

Hang Her in Laredo with Rita Hayworth was a flop. In the movie, they changed Maybelleen's name to Maria and made her a gun-toting Mexican revolutionary in love with a bandit named Mexicana Billy.

Maria eventually hangs for shooting the corrupt sheriff of Laredo. Of course at the end of the movie they realize that they hanged her by mistake and that they should have thanked her for killing the evil sheriff.

They turned the tornado into the wrath of God and all the townspeople into gamblers and prostitutes. The only part that was real was when they had Maybelleen land on the roof of the church. But then they turned her into an angel, complete with big white wings.

They just didn't get it.

After I found Maybelleen up there in the graveyard, she came to me often in dreams. I always knew she was there.

Then I grew up. I moved away and married Jack.

For a long time Maybelleen was quiet.

She was sleeping I think. Taking a rest.

I left Kentucky at twenty-one. I wanted to see what world lay out there past the soybean fields. I never took to farming.

I taught third grade in New York and wrote short stories at night. I got married and promised myself eternal happiness and decided I was a better teacher than a writer.

Life was mornings of green tea in blue china cups and laughing with Jack. I thought it would go on forever. Maybelleen melted away with my childhood and became a soft blur.

Then early one morning, I think it was in February, I woke up to frost on my windowpane and I realized that I was dissolving away into nothingness. That's when I knew I would leave no more tangible imprint on the world than the momentary ice on the glass of my bedroom window.

I fought this thing that grew and ate me inside. For every

thought of a blade on a wrist, I fought back with the thought of my husband's arms around me. I burrowed into his chest at night to follow the rhythm of his heart.

But it didn't work. I tried to listen to his heart because I couldn't hear mine at all.

One day Jack came home and found me dying. I can never remember it at all and when I think back to the scene as it must have looked, I've decided I must have read the whole thing in a book, for I've never been fascinated by blood and water. I'd always thought if I were to do it, I'd take some pills and dream myself to death.

From that time on I've worn these scars on my wrist and now I have them here, a necklace to match.

Scarred.

But Maybelleen comes to me now again in dreams and whispers. She's louder than before. I've heard her there in the corner of my peach room and seen her growing larger in the wallpaper. With each scar she comes closer.

She has something so important to tell me that it may even save my life. Or take it away. But whatever it is, she is blood of my blood and I'm listening for her even now in the hush of this September morning, a thousand miles away from what I had thought was my life.

Because you can't run away, can you? Life just chases you from here to there until at last it tracks you down. It manages to get from point A to B even if I can't.

Jack, that man who was to be old with me in a rocking chair, has never called or written. He has escaped from me without a single white hair.

Sometimes I wonder where he is. What he's thinking. Does he ever wonder what I'm doing? Does he ever wonder what I think?

I really did believe in love.

But now I'm home.

Yes, she says. Hush.

I can feel her arms around me in the dark. And the singular terrible loneliness I've always felt, melts away with her connection. There has to be a connection. And, it's in the blood.

"He's here," sings Aunt Opal from the bottom of the stairs. Oh my, I think. Oh my.

I haven't got a purse and I haven't got a comb.

But of course I do. And this man is down there waiting like an attendant to my continual confusion to take me somewhere in the green truck I see out the window, to someplace that I don't want to go. And my stomach is in knots.

"Margaret," she hollers.

"I'm coming," I say back, collecting my things, my purse, my sweater, all the things I thought I didn't have.

Maybelleen says nothing and the wallpaper is filled with flowers.

─❦◎

Now he's standing in the hallway, looking thin and nervous. When he looks at me and his eyes see mine, he doesn't smile.

"Well," says Aunt Opal, "you two have a lovely time. Sure you won't have a cup of coffee, Jim?"

"Thank you, no. The picture starts at seven-thirty and we've got a forty-minute ride."

"You have a wonderful time, honey," she says to me. She tips her face for a kiss. Her skin smells like peppermint tea and rosewater. She still hasn't found that box for me. The one with things from Maybelleen.

"You ready?" he asks me. But I shake my head. I think I should wear a hat of some kind and I don't like the scarf at my neck.

"Do you want an umbrella?" says Aunt Opal. "It's likely to rain."

He opens the front door and out I go. Stepping in front of him, feeling him at my back. What does he know, I wonder, because he does know something. And we're off to the movies in the big green truck.

The springs make a rusty, crunching sound and the seat bounces up and down. The road winds around to wherever we're going. I look out the window and even though leaves still hang onto the branches, to me it looks like winter.

He drives along quiet. The radio plays "Blueberry Hill" but the music doesn't fit comfortable inside this truck. We're too silent for this happy clap-along music.

I realize that this is the first time I've left the house except to go to the doctor once a week. The world's changed while I've been gone. It seems like just yesterday it was June and you heard the crickets scraping. Now it's cold and all those crickets are hiding beneath the ground.

"So," he finally says. "So. Miss New York?"

This wasn't what I was expecting. I thought it would go like, "So"—as he looks away—"feeling better?" or "Why'd you pull something like that anyway?"

But this man doesn't do anything I expect.

"New York," I say. The place now seems as far away as Cairo. When I look over at him, he's smiling. I never saw him smile before. His dark eyes get blacker.

"It's a big city. A place to get lost."

I don't smile back. It's as if my face is frozen as solid as the ground outside.

He turns down the radio. The lights on the dashboard glow phosphorescent.

"Biggest city I ever saw was Los Angeles."

I say nothing. Out the window I see birds wheeling in

the gloom, watching for something small to run across the open fields.

"We docked in San Diego, I was in the Navy, and me and a buddy went up on the train to see Hollywood."

The trees pass us by, cold air running visibly through their branches. I reach over and click the radio off. The music is too far from where we are. I catch a piece of my face in the glowing chrome of the dashboard as I lean to light my cigarette with the match he offers. He lights that match with just one hand. The other steers us firmly onward.

"Never saw any stars though," he says.

Now it's dark. We ride quiet for a few minutes, saying nothing, but there is this hum between us, so high that only a dog might hear it. We both look at each other at the same time and I say, "I went to New York to get away from the farm."

"You don't like farming?"

"Why, you do?"

"I got thirty acres I play with. Can't really call that a farm. My dad lost our place in 'forty-eight. Couldn't keep up the mortgage. I managed to buy back thirty acres of the four hundred we had."

"What do you raise?"

"Well, let's see. Last year, I put in ten in feed corn and tried the rest in tobacco, but I don't have the knack for it. I'm gonna let twenty lay fallow for a season and then try a new hybrid I worked out. Corn. Comes out almost pink and it's the sweetest-tastin' corn you ever ate."

He scratches his thigh and yawns. He pats the steering wheel with the palm of his hand in time to some music in his head.

We're quiet the rest of the way. The sound of the truck thrums through the cab. It's steady and sure. I can picture the pistons under the hood gleaming silver and mighty.

We buy popcorn and Bon Bons and Jujubes. We were going to see *Cat on a Hot Tin Roof* but the line was too long so we ended up here, sitting down after the credits had rolled.

We had to find seats in the dark and feel out our places with our hands filled. He spilled most of the popcorn and I dropped my Coke.

He laughed.

The movie was called *Gun Glory* with Stewart Granger. It was about a gunfighter who quits. I didn't believe a second of it. When the lights came up, I had popcorn scattered all around my lap. He helped me brush myself off and we went for a drink.

He put his arm around me as we walked from the theater up the street to the bar.

"This okay?"—as he pointed to the sign—"Five Spot Lounge."

He orders a whiskey and soda for himself. "What will you have?"

"I'm on medication," I say. "But I'll have a gin and tonic."

"Whoa!" he says. "Hold on there, Nellie!"

"I'm not a horse and that's what I want."

He nods and looks at me with those night-black eyes. He doesn't say it, he catches himself but I see it. "It's your funeral," is what he'd have said ordinarily.

"Look," I say, the drink giving me wings. "What the hell is this all about?"

"What?" He runs his hand through his hair. He does that all the time, I notice. It's his little quirk, like my chewing on my index cuticle.

"What do you want me for? And I'll have another drink."

"Sure." He motions the short-skirted waitress over.

I drink it like I'm thirstier than I know and I feel lights coming on in my head.

"What were you doing in my hospital room? Why'd you come there? What do you want? Do you know, I sometimes felt you? I even dreamed you were an angel of some sort, though I don't believe in God. It seemed you were this dark angel come to get me.

"Never mind," I say.

I look around me for something to anchor my thoughts. A jukebox stands in the corner gleaming with blue-and-red lights.

His eyes never flicker away from mine and he answers none of my questions.

"Play you something?" he asks.

"Oh, play anything."

He walks over to the jukebox and his back is thin. I don't know how he manages to look big at all with such a thin back. And his skin underneath his farmer's red tan is white as feathers.

He sits back down trailing a song behind him. "I don't know a damn thing about music, but I always liked this song.

> " 'I turned and tossed until it seemed you had gone
> but here you are with the dawn.
> Wish I'd forget you, but you're here to stay.'

"Kind of sums it up." He beckons and the waitress brings him another drink.

"You can't sing," I say.

"Never said I could."

So we're quiet. The jukebox keeps playing Billie Holiday. He sips his drink. I look at other women's hairdos. I realize that I probably look like hell.

"I became a deputy sheriff when my ma died, couple of years ago. I didn't have anyone left, well, I got a sister but she's out in California now. I thought about going to New

York or Chicago. The farm was gone and I wasn't married. But what could I have done?

"Anyway, my dad was good friends with the sheriff and after a while, when it seemed all I was good for was gettin' in bar fights and livin' like a bum, he offered me the job and I took it."

I circle my glass around on the table. I don't look at him. I don't know why he's telling me this. I don't want to hear.

"So I got my life in order. Bought the acreage. Thought I had it all figured out neat and clean until I climbed up into that hayloft and saw you stretched out in the hay."

He lifts my chin and his skin is rough as rope.

"I saw your face."

What am I supposed to say now? What is he telling me? "So?"

"I don't know," he says. He slams down his glass. "I don't know either. But I've got things to do and your face is constantly in front of me."

"Getting in the way?"

His eyes look at me so deep and dark that I have to look away.

"Maybe," he says.

And something tumbles over inside me.

"I'm nuts, you know."

"Shit," he says. "You're not nuts. You're nowhere near it. I've seen nuts. You ever been out to Evenston Hospital?

That's nuts, honey, and you're nowhere near. No. Now, you listen here. You are just plain scared of something and you're running away. That's all it is."

"I'm manic-depressive. It's hereditary."

"Bullshit."

"My great-aunt was crazy."

"My great-aunt was a Bible teacher and I don't teach Sunday school."

"Look," I say, "thank you. I appreciate your vote of confidence. You're a nice guy. You really are. You should be dating some pretty girl who'd just love to raise corn with you. Can you take me home now?"

"Sure."

The whole way back we're truly silent. There is no hum between us, nothing at all. He's right. I'm not nuts. I always knew that anyway.

In front of my aunt and uncle's he drops me off, keeps the engine running. I pull up on the silver handle.

"I'll be in touch."

"To check up on me?"

"Nope," he says. "Why don't you check up on yourself?"

I slam the door and sail past Aunt Opal and her offering of hot tea.

I climb into the blankets and search everywhere for her.

There's nothing but myself.

I take two pills instead of one. I don't want any dreams at all.

Why can't he just leave me alone?

He's chased her clean away.

Maybelleen
1900
Oklahoma Territory

"Please call me Elias in front of people, Maybelleen. Not Dr. Brown. It sounds so . . . like I'm old as the hills. You know these people look up to me and therefore also to you, as my wife."

"Of course," said Maybelleen. "I thought you'd appreciate it is all, all those scarecrows gathered like vultures at the church, making such a big deal of your 'mission.' The good Dr. Brown, the holy Dr. Brown and your fawning converts, pawing you for favors. And anyway, let's be realistic. I'm the one as old as the hills. You're Dr. Charm."

"And baking the cake with salt! Maybelleen, why did you do it? Poor Mrs. Ladersall got quite sick."

"Oh, I made a mistake is all. Sugar. Salt. They look the same. See?" Maybelleen held up two glass jars to the doctor filled with identical white stuff. "Which is which? And she didn't have to wolf the cake down like a starved pig, did she?"

"Maybelleen, it's hard enough. The wives think that you're . . ."

"Crazy? No, that's not it." She puffed her lips and blew the stray hair out of her face. "Not crazy. I just thought there was more to it, is all."

"More to what? I don't understand you more than half the time anymore."

"Pooh." She pulled a mixing bowl off a rough wooden shelf.

"Maybelleen, you have to understand what it is we're up against these days. The government constantly undermines all we try to do. You may despise my fellows, call them scarecrows or whatever you wish, but my dear, what do you think would happen if there were no one here to try to help the poor Indians?"

"From what I've seen these past eight months, it seems that just about everyone has got it all wrong. I think we should all go away and leave them alone. Let them war whoop. Let them dance. Let them do whatever it is that they want to do. Did you bring the flour?"

"It comes in Thursday. But you can't deny the work we've

done, May, for God's sake! Look at the school the Mission has built you, look at the tools given to you out of sheer love!"

"Or out of guilt. Elias, I don't want to start this again. I'm tired. I'm just plain tired. How am I supposed to bake all that bread without flour?"

"Maybelleen, Maybelleen, dearest heart, please don't sound this way. It hurts me, it stabs me as clean through as though you'd taken a knife to my breast and pushed it through. And what do you think it does to the Indians? Do you think they're helped by your bitterness? I don't understand how you've changed."

"Oh Elias, for Christ's sake, can't you at least drop this sham when we're alone?"

"Maybelleen! What sham? Do you think that I simply playact in my role as minister here? Do you think I take this responsibility lightly?"

"You know, I really don't know the answer to that. I know that you certainly take yourself seriously. Now, please, Elias, leave me be. No, don't start that now, I'm in no mood. I have to get this bread done for your self-reliant Indians in the morning. Since I don't have the heavenly connections that you have, I don't know how I'm going to perform that miracle with this little flour."

Maybelleen turned away from her husband and looked out the thick glass windowpane. The doctor stared down at the hand that had stroked his wife's breast as though it were a spider.

She didn't really know why she talked to him this way. She only knew that it was the easiest thing to do. Outside the little house, the dirt street separated them from the white church. The sky was blue but through the window it appeared gray. Everything was always covered with dust.

"It's not our fault that they opened the Territory."

"No? You and your wonderful friends. You and the wonderful idea of land for the Indians. Well, give it to them and take it away. Your hero, Mr. Dawes, he's the one responsible."

"It's surplus land, dear. You just don't understand."

"Surplus? Because they weren't farming like the good people in Ohio? Well, of course. If they aren't using it then take it away! It just makes me sick. Oh, it makes me sick." She pulled bottles out of the cupboard, looking for the port.

"You don't know what you're talking about, May, and you're in no condition. You've worked yourself into a passion. You were never like this. If we had a child, as I've said before . . ."

"The sad thing is, Elias, you don't know what you're talking about. And leave me alone about a baby. I didn't choose it. We've tried. And how do you know what I'm like or ever was?" She pulled the cork from the port and poured some in a tin coffee cup.

"Now leave me be. Now that I'm here, I'm certainly not

going to let them starve. Your plan for making them all good citizens has left them with nothing, and in case you hadn't noticed, most of them live on mush because government beef can't be trusted not to kill you."

"Maybelleen, that's enough of that kind of talk. I won't have it in this house!"

"Go away, Elias." Maybelleen turned away from her husband. She waited for him to leave but he didn't. She knew he stood there still, just waiting for something from her. She turned back and his hair got caught in a ray of sunlight and made a halo about his face. She felt bad then, for he did mean the things he said even if they were the wrong things.

Since she had married him his eyes had constant bags beneath them and his handsome profile had begun to droop.

"I wish you wouldn't drink that," he said. "It just makes things worse."

"Why don't you work on your sermon?" she said. "Go on. Go do God's work. Go do it well and maybe you'll get called back East. Just concentrate on all those sinners drinking and dancing in Chicago."

They stared at each other until he dropped his eyes.

"Of course, dear. I think that I'll go and finish my sermon."

"Do that."

He left the small kitchen. Behind him rose the sound of blows as Maybelleen punched at what he hoped was the bread dough.

In the corner of the bedroom, the doctor put his head in his hands. "My Lord do not forsake me in the wilderness," he said. But even as he said this he felt as though he were an actor in a play with the wrong ending.

From the kitchen Maybelleen sang, "Oh, I wish I was in the land of cotton, old times there are not forgotten, look away, look away."

"In the wilderness of my wife's desertion. For she has left me, Lord, as surely as if she had run away." Tears rolled down his face for he felt very sorry for himself. Just look at what was happening to his wonderful career. And they'd forgotten him in Chicago. They were going to leave him in this godforsaken place forever.

"Dixie land!" she sang as loudly as her lungs allowed, "Look away, Dixie land."

"I think she's mad," he said to his opened Bible. "I don't know what to do." He wished so badly that he really could believe. He would have to suffer more. He knew that but was so terrified. He hated pain and suffering, it wasn't his forte. People should listen to him with shining eyes but the people here were ignoramuses.

"I got a mule and her name is Sal, I drink all day and all night."

Perhaps he should take her back to Kentucky.

"And when I'm drunk, I'm a total skunk. La dee doo da day!"

~❀◉

For three months Maybelleen taught Cheyenne children in the schoolhouse built by the Presbyterian Mission. Most of the Arapahos had been stolen by the Lutherans.

During the day in the one room, boys to the left, girls to the right, she would repeat, "*A* is for apple, *B* is for button." She drew upon a chalkboard all of the states of the union. "Indiana, Kentucky, Idaho, California. This is the flag of the United States. You are Americans." The children repeated whatever she told them to. They were good children.

Dr. Brown didn't think so. Neither did most of his fellow missionaries. Although they didn't come out and say it, Maybelleen saw that they judged the children's worth by how clean they were and how obedient. The good Indian children were the ones who did what they were told without asking why.

Good Dr. Brown.

One Monday morning—it was very early and cold and the wood had not yet taken in the stove—she sat at her oak desk and looked out at the empty classroom. The children that would soon file in, feet dragging like children anywhere, would take her mind away from the mistake she'd made for one more day.

She was an excellent teacher. Two students, Boy Running

from Dogs and Falls Down in Rain were truly gifted. Their names now, of course, were Sam and Clara.

Clara's mother worked for Susan Griegs out at Fort Reno in the Presbyterian mission there and Clara hadn't seen her for two years. Clara lived with her father, Joe Two Cloud, in a one-room shack on the reservation two miles from the school. Joe Two Cloud said he was a chief and the Indian police were always arresting him for shooting his guns off at passing dogs, carts, and old men. Joe Two Cloud drank a lot, it was said. He was very old and Clara—Falls Down in Rain—was his only living child.

Maybelleen heard him one day outside the schoolhouse screaming, something that sounded like a snake hiss. "Tis-Tsis-Tas" he went over and over again.

The children got up from their seats and pressed their faces against the windows to see him. Then Clara went outside and took him home to the reservation.

"What was he yelling, Clara?" Maybelleen asked her the next day.

"Our name," she said. "The People. He is ashamed because he didn't go on the long march with Dull Knife and Little Wolf and now he lives like an old dog on a chain. That's what he tells me."

"Oh," Maybelleen had said to the serious nine-year-old. "I'm sorry."

"Don't worry, Mrs. Brown," she'd said. "Soon he'll die."

"Well, that's not good," she'd said to the girl.

"Oh yes it is. Then he'll be happy."

Her other prize pupil, Sam, was an orphan. His mother and father died of malaria. His grandmother was her husband's prize Christian and she kept a house that ran wild with morning glories and nasturtiums. She raised chickens and sold them and made down quilts and pillows. The grandmother had decided that Sam would be a minister, like her hero, Dr. Elias Brown.

Sam had confided in Maybelleen, however, that he wanted to be a rancher. He wanted to raise cattle.

Maybelleen didn't ask him where or how he proposed to do this. As far as land allotment was concerned, no one was clear anymore what land the Cheyenne had any right to, least of all the Cheyenne. It all seemed to change from day to day. It was certain, however, that the land ceded to these people in a small corner of Oklahoma Territory was definitely not conducive to Sam's idea of ranching.

Maybelleen thought of these two children as she sat there in the cold square room at six o'clock on Monday morning and tried to fill herself up with their promise. She shivered and put several more sticks in the stove. She rubbed her back where it ached and remembered she had another birthday coming.

A birthday.

She couldn't get pregnant. She was hollow as a log inside.

Ever since they had arrived in the little town of New Jerusalem she had felt her soul shrinking day by day.

On Sundays there was church or the entire day, her husband beaming from his ornate cherry pulpit, lifting his hands to the heavens and praying every Indian to a white and gold heaven.

On Tuesdays there was a "social," when all the neighboring missionaries came together at the Browns' for punch and cookies and the planning of the welfare of their Indians.

No Indians were invited to attend.

On Thursday there was Bible study over which her husband presided in their kitchen and on Saturday there was the "visiting."

At first she had gone eagerly with her husband. They went to visit the Indians on the reservation and they brought Bibles and cakes and pies. She had badly wanted to see how these people lived and had wanted very much to know them. But after the first few visits she wondered if her husband was blind to the glances that the men gave him as he patted the heads of their children and talked to them of Jesus. She saw the women hang their heads as he preached the sin of alcohol to their husbands. She winced when he tossed aside an offered horn-handled knife and lectured the giver about Cain and Abel. And she turned and marched away from the reservation on the day that he halted a dance by kicking the drums helter-skelter in the dust.

"Maybelleen," he'd cried as he'd finally overtaken her. "Maybelleen, they must stop these pagan things and come into the world!"

"Leave me alone," she'd said that day. She'd never again stepped foot on the reservation. She had married a man who found dancing a sin.

She stood when she heard the voices outside the schoolhouse, heard the words they said and the words were not English.

"What am I doing?" she said to the map of the world spread out in full, glorious color on the wall.

When all the children were seated she stood up and said, "Today we will do something different and perhaps we'll do something different forever. Today, I want you to teach me something; today, I will be your student, children.

"George, yes, you. Come up here."

The fourteen-year-old stood and came slowly up to Maybelleen. He was a big boy, almost six feet tall, and learned slowly. He seldom smiled and his clothes were often filthy. She knew nothing of his parents. He would scarcely talk at all and the other children seemed to stay out of his way. He came to school every day, however, even through snow. He was always accompanied by a small yellow dog. The dog would wait outside for George to come out and then Maybelleen would see them walking away together toward the reservation. She never saw George touch the dog or even speak to it, yet it walked at his side as though they were the best of friends.

Dr. Brown had told Maybelleen that the Cheyenne ate dogs and didn't keep them as pets. But it didn't look to her as though George was planning on eating the little yellow dog. It seemed to her as though they had more of an understanding between the two of them than her husband and his fellows had of George and his people.

"Now, here, sit here at my desk," Maybelleen said to George. "I will sit at yours. Go on, sit down."

The children giggled as the tall boy slowly sat down in the teacher's chair.

"What's the matter, George?"

"It ain't right, Mrs. Brown."

"Nonsense. It is right. It's time we all learned something important. Now are you comfortable?"

The boy nodded slowly. A child clapped.

"Now, George. Tell us a story. It's a new day and a new class. Tell us a story about, how do you say it Clara? Tis-Tas?"

"Tis-Tsis-Tas."

"What does that mean, children?"

One boy shook his head as Maybelleen looked at him, another grinned.

"Tell them, Clara."

"It is our name. It means the People."

"Yes," said Maybelleen. "Now, George, tell us a story of the Tis-Tsis-Tas."

The boy leaned back in the hardwood chair. "I don't know. . . . No. Don't know no story." He looked down at the desk.

The children laughed.

"Dummy," said one boy.

"Can't even talk good," said another.

"Come, George," said Maybelleen. "All you children hush. George speaks very well. All of you speak beautifully. I guess the teacher before me must have drilled and drilled you. I only wish I could speak your language as you speak mine. There's nothing wrong with making mistakes. How do we learn? Now, George, I know that you have a story and a good one too."

"The other teacher used to beat George with a big stick," said Clara.

"Well that was stupid," said Maybelleen.

George looked out at the eighteen boys and girls. They were staring at him. "Alright," he said. "This is a story from my grandmother and you had all better listen good."

"They will," said Maybelleen. The children quieted.

"Many many years ago, before now and before our beautiful teacher, Mrs. Brown, was here, we were not here."

"I know the story!" said a girl.

"Be quiet, Susan. Go on, George."

The boy stared hard at Maybelleen. "This here is the real story, Mrs. Brown. Once we had another God. He wasn't Jesus, he was greater than Jesus."

The boy looked at Maybelleen and she nodded her head. The boy stood up behind the desk. He picked up the chalk and on the chalkboard he drew trees and water and flowers. "Once our God made the world. He was a Great Spirit, greater than all the saints in the Bible. He made the sun and the stars and he made all the plants and animals. He made a place far to the north that was the most beautiful place. It was more beautiful than heaven.

"There were all kinds of animals and the People lived with them and they could all talk to one another. They were all friends."

"That's true!" said a boy. "My grandpa, he told me."

"Our God made three kinds of humans. One kind that was hairy all over, one kind that was white and had hair on their heads and faces, and one kind that was red and had hair only on their heads. The hairy people were very strong, the white people were like wolves and were tricky and cunning like wolves are, and the red people were fast runners and the Great Spirit taught them to eat fish, to catch them and eat them and nobody else knew how to do that.

"Well, the hairy people left the beautiful land and went

south and the red people followed them. But before they went the Great Spirit got them all together and told them how to make things, like arrows and spears and pots and things like that they might need.

"Nobody knows what happened to the hairy people. They went to live in caves and were afraid to come out but the red people always stayed together. Finally they went back to their beautiful land but they found they couldn't talk to the animals anymore, the white people were all gone and the Great Spirit, our God, told them to leave because there was going to be a big huge flood.

"So they did. And there was a flood. But after the water disappeared they went back to their beautiful land but it wasn't beautiful anymore. There weren't any trees, no animals, no fish. And the People cried.

"But now the People had become divided up; they spoke different languages. They learned from the Great Spirit how to hunt. He gave them buffalo and corn and they lived in the south always after that but they never forgot their beautiful land to the north."

George stood in front of the class and pointed.

"Now all of you listen. Now the People are divided again. We live here and we live in the north. Some went up north to our old hunting grounds but some stayed. Never again will the People be allowed to be all together. This has happened because we are punished by the whites for killing Long Hair

Custer and for being proud. So, we live here and we die but we know that someday we will go to the beautiful country and we will never forget it no matter what they tell us."

The children stared at the boy. Maybelleen took a deep breath. The boy's face was lighted from inside. Then Maybelleen clapped and the children clapped.

Then, one clapped like this: *clap, clap clap clap, clap*. They all clapped like drums together. "Hey," sang out one girl; "Hey nah," sang another.

Maybelleen stood, clapping, her foot tapping. The boy, George, beat time on the wood of the desk. "Dance!" cried Maybelleen. "Let's all dance!" and the children looked at one another for only a moment and then Clara bent over, her two hands over her head, and went this way and that to the lovely beat. Another child followed, and another. Sam leaped into the air and the boys followed him, dancing between the rows.

Maybelleen led them around the room, the children chanting and singing. She raised her arms and sang words she didn't understand but that didn't matter.

"What is this!" said a voice, but Maybelleen didn't hear it in the singing dance, in the pulse of the music, until a noise so loud and unrhythmic halted the dancers in mid-step.

"Mrs. Brown, what on earth are you doing? Have you lost your mind?"

They were all quiet before Dr. Brown. They stood there

together with silent hands and feet and stared at him and then at their teacher.

"No, Elias, I've found my mind. We are simply learning to understand one another."

"Well that's quite enough. Mrs. Brown, please stop hopping about. Take the buggy and go home and lie down. I will take over the class today."

"Elias—"

Dr. Brown slammed a desk again with his buggy whip. "That's enough, Mrs. Brown. I've had quite enough. Do you understand me? Now, do not make me angry in front of these children. You are undoing everything that I've labored so hard for!"

Maybelleen, gone white, put on her jacket and picked up her books. Then the little girl, Clara, came up to her and took her hand. "Good-bye, Mrs. Brown," she said.

"Sit down, girl," said Dr. Brown.

"Good-bye, Clara," said Maybelleen. "I will miss you all."

"This is how it always is," said Clara. "But don't worry Mrs. Brown, George's story was true. It's true."

"Sit down!" bellowed Dr. Brown. "I will have obedience!"

Outside Maybelleen gathered the reins of the horse and turned the buggy toward the house the missionary society had built for them. She passed it to the left and continued on toward the Canadian River, the ruts in the road jarring her spine and belly. She didn't know where she was going but she was going away from Dr. Elias Brown and his probing night hands, his visions of hell, his version of truth.

"Maybelleen can't you love me?" came his voice after her on the rocky road. "Can't you love me? What is wrong? I only try to do what's right, Maybelleen, I'm only human. I try to do what's right."

But it isn't right she thought. None of it is. People were made to dance and tell stories. Not made to groan and moan above a woman and then lash themselves with a belt buckle. But still he'd beg, "Can't you love me? Can't you love me?"

What had happened to this man, she wondered. The confident Dr. Brown from the ladies' literary tea had become a man who lied to the Indians he claimed to love, a man who lied, worst of all, to himself.

Maybelleen cried. She cried hard. It stopped up her nose and blinded her so that she dropped the reins to cry some more.

She'd thought she was smart, marrying Dr. Brown, getting away from Kentucky, going somewhere far away from the darkness inside her but it wasn't any different. Not at all.

Now she sat in the middle of a road broken in dry crumbled chunks. The air was frozen around her. Her heart was frozen inside her. She was far away from dreaming about being far away. She didn't see the horses coming fast, hear them coming around the little turn ahead of where she sat crying for all her lostness.

She was so very afraid of herself. She felt as small as small can be.

She never saw the horse that slipped and hit the little buggy. She did see her horse as it reared up and sideways. Then they both fell so very slowly to the cold ripped ground.

Maybelleen MacGregor Brown was alone in Oklahoma Territory bleeding from the head, knocked senseless until the horse who'd hit the buggy came back and the rider looked down and saw her.

"Pick her up," that rider had said.

But Maybelleen couldn't hear him.

"But what the hell, Bill! What we gonna do with her?"

"Pick her up, put her here." And the black man had lifted her up, her blood soaking his bright blue shirt. He'd lifted her to the other rider's saddle and that man had shifted and twisted her and held her tight.

"Let's go, Bill!" said another man as he grabbed May-belleen's dancing mare from the traces of the trap. "Jesus God, let's go!" He mounted his horse, pulling Maybelleen's mare behind.

Maybelleen nearly slipped away many times as the three rode into the dark, until they came to a shack outside of the town of Rain.

It was getting dark as the man laid Maybelleen down on the dirt floor. He washed the blood from her head.

"She got a big knot," said the black man. "Let's take her over to the reservation and leave her there."

"Shut up, Vitus," said the other man. "I done this and had to come back 'cause it weren't right to leave a woman bleeding in the dirt. It weren't right then and it ain't right now."

"Bill, sometimes I think you're looney as a wild goat. You think they ain't gonna come lookin' for her? Shit, they's lookin' for us already! And we didn't even get the damn money. You ain't God, Bill."

"How do you know, Vitus?" he said.

The man lit a kerosene lamp and set it on the floor. The flame made shadows climb the walls. "Cover the window," said the man. "Who's to say where God is anyway? For all you know I'm all there is in the God department."

"Doubt it," said the other man. His name was Shoe. "If'n you are, why don't ya heal me?" He held his clubfoot in the other man's face and shook it. He laughed. "Vitus, you ain't got no spirit at all! Why Bill here, he took us on a lark today. Maybe we ain't got the money but we sure as hell had the fun, ya sour ol' cuss. Hell, outlawin' is somethin' you ain't never gonna understand."

Mexican Bill looked down at Maybelleen then covered her with his saddle blanket.

"And she's ugly too!" said the clubfoot.

"We can't get her no help tonight," said Bill, "so's we'll have to watch her. We'll take her over to the doc in Rain in the morning and leave her there for her folks."

"Damn and all," said Black Vitus. "Ridin' with you, Bill, is no doubt hairier than ever it was with Jack Pershing, that's no lie. But at least Jack got the gold off'n the trains more times than not and he weren't half as smart as a hatbox. Here you is, so smart and all and we ain't got enough to buy us a steak dinner in Leadville."

"Jack Pershing also got a rope 'round his neck," said the other man with the built-up shoe.

"Neither one of you needs to ride with me if'n you don't wanna. I never asked neither of you to. If you both wanna ride clean outta here now, then get goin'. I'm stayin' till mornin' 'cause I can't think of a better place to go right now."

"Mad as a bee in a jelly jar. Crazy as a Mexican bedbug," said Shoe. "How you figure on takin' her to the doc when they's no doubt federal marshals circlin' all around here like buzzards? Think them boys care whether them folks got robbed or not? I'll tell ya, I seen folks hanged for makin' too much noise on a Sunday. Them was the ol' days, I reckon. Still and all, you's buildin' yourself a reputation for stupidity, Bill, and that's a true hangin' offense in most counties. Takin' in women. Damn. I never. Givin' good money to Injuns for nothin'. You're a regular Robin what's-his-name. Only I heard he had some brains." He laid out his bedroll and climbed inside. "But what the hell, I say. I'm in for the fun is all."

"I don't know that I'm stayin', Bill," said Vitus.

Mexican Bill said nothing. He sat there on the cold dirt floor staring at the gray wood of the shack.

"Vitus, youse too old and too tired to go anyplace. You know that. Let's get some sleep," said Shoe.

"Mebbe I could if'n you'd shut your yap. We still hittin' Judgment?" asked Vitus.

Bill watched the woman on the ground. He wondered if she was awake and just pretending to sleep.

"Well, are we?"

"Sure, we'll hit Judgment," said Shoe. "That's the big plan. Don't you never listen? Won't we Bill? In an' out like lightnin'. Grab the loot and hightail it."

"We hit Judgment tomorrow," said Bill. "Now everybody shut up and let me think."

"Oh you sure is a saint there, Bill. Helpin' women in need. You figure that's gonna keep you outta hell?"

Mexican Bill pulled a book out of his coat.

"You still readin' that book, Bill?"

But Mexican Bill just turned another page.

"I went to the woods because I wished to live deliberately, to front only the essential facts of life, and see if I could not learn what it had to teach, and not, when I came to die, discover that I had not lived."

He read very slowly because he didn't read well. He had to go over things many times and sort the words out loud. At the Catholic boys' school in South Texas, he'd been a poor student.

"Still we live meanly, like ants; though the fable tells us that we were long ago changed into men; like pygmies we fight with cranes; . . ."

"I don't see why that Walden fella didn't come out west. Then he'd have gotten the whole thing straight," said Shoe. "Why I lived in Philadelphia until I was old enough to run away and fight the Rebs. I was just fourteen."

"Oh shut up with your damn stories," said Vitus from his blanket. "Somebody's gotta get some sleep aroun' here. Somebody's gotta be able to think straight."

"Still, that Walden fella wouldn't have had to write that book at all if'n he'd just gone west. From what you've read me, Bill, that man was just confused, mixin' up fancy words and all. Don't see why you gotta be readin' it."

Shoe continued on for a while. Mexican Bill ignored him. "All that posh about rabbits and squirrels . . ."

Mexican Bill glanced down at the woman and she was staring right into his eyes.

"Are you hurtin'?" he asked her.

She just stared and he wondered as he looked, what it was that she saw. If she saw the same thing that he did.

In the little new-made town of New Jerusalem, Dr. Elias Brown came home to a dark and empty house.

"Maybelleen?" he called out.

The oven was cold and the buggy was gone. He looked out back for the horse but it wasn't there.

"Come on!" he told the searchers later, the Indians and the missionaries. "We must find her! Look everywhere, men. Find her!"

It wasn't long until they found the buggy—overturned and its struts bent. The horse was nowhere around.

"Blood here," said an Indian.

"Jehoshaphat!" said Mr. Lemon. "She's been kidnapped."

"Abducted?" Dr. Brown looked about the spot wonderingly as if the ground might have swallowed his wife.

"No ducks," said the Indian.

"Who would kidnap a woman?" asked Dr. Brown.

"Indians," said Mr. Lemon. Mr. Lemon kept the dry-goods store and was a practical man who believed in a God of hell and high water and keeping Indians as far away from him as possible. Now he shoved the Cheyenne away from Dr. Brown's side. "Indians abduct 'em."

The Cheyenne shrugged. "No ducks here," he repeated.

"Of course there ain't no ducks, man. The woman's been kidnapped. *Comprende?* Taken away." He waved his hands in the air. "Oh what's the use with these people. Well, Dr. Brown, we'll simply have to put together a posse. That's how to find her."

"A posse?"

"Let's see, there's me and you. John Stewart, you'll ride with us. . . ."

John Stewart nodded.

"And Samuel Breckeridge and Joe Shannon."

"But the sheriff," said Dr. Brown.

"The sheriff's all the way down to Rain. By the time we get ahold of him, your woman'll be dead, I can guarantee it. I seen this before in 'seventy-eight in Montana. Yep, likely she's been taken by Indians."

"No Indian would take a white woman," said the Cheyenne. "Don't take women at all. Don't need to. There are tracks here of three horses—"

Mr. Lemon hit the man in the face with his whip. "We didn't ask you."

"Now, now," said Dr. Brown. "Please. I must think."

The Cheyenne looked Mr. Lemon over. "You find the

woman. But it's not Indians that took her. No Indian would want a damn white woman."

"Samuel, don't leave, we need you," said Dr. Brown. "Lemon, you shouldn't have hit him."

The four Cheyenne talked a moment among themselves, mounted their horses, and rode away.

"We don't need him," said Mr. Lemon. "Like as not, they're in on it too. Now look, we'll find them all and hang 'em from the nearest tree."

"Oh please, that's ridiculous. Now, just wait." Dr. Brown got down from his horse and looked at the frozen ground. "It's difficult to make out, I do see a horse hoof here and here. I don't know," said Dr. Brown. "I wish I knew what to do. Mr. Lemon, please. And Samuel Two Bird is a good Christian, I'm certain that none of them had a thing to do with it. Let's be civilized here. Rationality. That's what this calls for. First we'll pray and then—"

"Pray all you want, Dr. Brown. All I know is a woman's been kidnapped by Indians and I for one have had enough of their drunken, murderous ways."

So, Mr. Lemon did all the organizing. It was as if he'd done it all before. "The first place to look is the reservation," he said. "Though they've likely got her holed up somewheres else."

"I'll agree she's gone," said Dr. Brown, "and I'll thank you men to just help me find her."

When the five men met later it was dark as black coffee. Clouds covered the stars and Dr. Brown held a kerosene lamp to light the way over the frozen ground. The horses stumbled in the ruts and their breath blew white in the night air.

"She'll be the death of me," said Dr. Brown. He sat awkwardly on his horse. The Winchester kept poking him in the groin and wouldn't stay put.

"Ooohee, Dr. Brown, now that's a gun," said Lemon when they'd gathered in front of the church. "Winchester lever action, huh? Well, we'll pump 'em."

"It was a present," said Dr. Brown, "from the Chicago Fire Association. I've never used it and I have no intention of doing so."

"What's that?"

"Nothing, Mr. Lemon. Nothing. I just think this is a bit far-fetched is all. I'm only coming along because I fear she's run away. I was a bit hard on her today and she may have hit her head. She's probably somewhere around here, wandering around dazed. I don't think she's kidnapped at all. She just had an accident."

"We'll see about that," said Lemon, pulling his knit cap down on his head. "I know how you feel, Brown, about your Indians. I know you don't want to believe the worst. But I'm sayin' it's pretty unlikely that your wife run off on account of you said a few harsh words, though we all know Mrs.

Brown's a bit strange in the head. Still, where'd the tracks of three horses stomped all around that buggy come from? Now you think about it, Brown. Who else'd do it 'round here? Time to stop this Indian nonsense once and for all."

"That's right," said Joe Shannon. "Enough's enough."

Enough of what? thought Dr. Brown. But he was tired and hadn't had his dinner so he dropped the thought way down deep. "I don't like this," was all he said. "I don't like this one bit."

But still he rode on behind the other four, wondering where she could be. He was convinced she was making him suffer and he didn't like it one bit. She was not keeping up her promise to be a helpmate, she was simply putting him through hell. Well, she'd find the shoe on the other foot when he found her. That, he decided, was a promise.

But the thought of her wandering cold and lost through a dark country brought new tears to his eyes. "Oh May," he said inside. "You can sing and dance all you want, just be alright."

"My baby," she said to him.

"What?" he said.

"Oh," she said, and shook her head. "I was dreaming, I think, of a little baby."

The man was an Indian, she saw. The light hurt her eyes and she had to close them again.

She turned her head and it ached. "Where are we?"

"Outside of Rain," said Mexican Bill.

Maybelleen looked again at the man who was looking at her. Something seemed to punch her direct in the chest, she had to take such a deep breath she nearly choked on the air. His face was so familiar yet she'd never seen him before.

Everything inside her felt out of kilter. The man looked at her with eyes so soft they were like a blanket. He smoothed back her hair from her face. She was so tired. Thoughts tilted and twirled and flashed in her head.

"Sleep," said the man.

"Are you crying?" she asked.

She fell asleep before he answered.

"Well," said Shoe. "That's done it."

"What?" said Vitus.

"Now he's gone and talked to her. Ol' Robin here."

Mexican Bill stood up and looked down at the two old men. "I'm thinkin'."

"Well, think away, Billy boy. Think away. Ow!" he said as *Walden Pond* came flying into his forehead. "Damn! It makes a better weapon than a read though."

"What?" said Mexican Bill.

He was pacing the little floor.

"Aw nothin'. It just ain't like the ol' days is all."

"That's good, you ol' croakers," said Mexican Bill. "'Cause this is the new days, fellas."

⁓❀◎

"Halt!" came the voice, and Dr. Brown reined in. Lemon leaned over and said, "I'll do the talkin'. It's a lawman, that's all. I'll get rid of him."

"Well it's about time we had the law, Lemon."

"What do you want?" asked the voice.

"Who are you?" said Lemon.

"Who are you?"

"We're out after his wife is what it is. She's been kidnapped by Indians is all. So's we've got a posse here to find their thievin' asses and give 'em you know what."

"Well, give it up, boys, this here is a federal posse and we don't need no tinhorns gettin' in the way."

"You found her?" asked Lemon.

"Who?" said the marshal.

"His wife, ya nitwit. Ya found the damned redskins that taken her? Damn, they left tracks. Three horses back there, what else you out here for?"

"Who you callin' a nitwit?" said the marshal. "This is government business."

"Excuse me, Marshal. Mr. Lemon here is a bit excited. You see, my wife appears to be missing. We found her buggy overturned and her horse gone—"

"And she's been kidnapped by redskins," said Joe Shannon.

"Now, that's not true," said Dr. Brown. "Mr. Lemon here is simply a bit overeager."

"Just a minute," said the marshal. He turned his horse back to a campfire where two other men sat drinking coffee.

"Good thing," said Dr. Brown. "They'll get to the bottom of this thing."

"Aw, they ain't gonna do nothin'," said Lemon. "'Cept find her and send the Indians to some nice cushy federal farm. That's how come they don't never learn nothin'. Treat 'em like soft-bottomed babies."

The marshal signaled the group to dismount and join the others at the campfire.

"Here's how it is, boys. Now me and my men are out after Mexican Bill and his bunch. They hit the bank in Curleyville yesterday and the feed store in Wolf Hollow last week. They're holed up around here, we've got 'em tracked straight through the reservation. We figure they're headin' for Wichita till things cool off.

"Now, you say you seen tracks of three horses where your wife's buggy was found?"

"That's right, Marshal," said Dr. Brown.

"That's the number," said the marshal. "Where exactly was that buggy?"

"About six miles back on the road out of New Jerusalem. What exactly are you saying, Marshal? Do you think these outlaws might have Maybelleen?"

"Doesn't figure, exactly. I mean what would they want with your wife? It isn't Bill's modus operandi, if you know what I mean. But Bill isn't exactly your run-of-the-mill outlaw."

"Is he a killer, Marshal?" Dr. Brown was perspiring heavily. The thought of Maybelleen walking around frozen, dazed, and repentant was what was keeping him going. He didn't believe the Indian nonsense for a moment. But outlaws. That was ghastly and horrible. "Why would they want her? Whatever for?"

"Well that doesn't make any sense at all. Don't figure Bill'd want to be rapin' her. Never heard of him doing that. But you never know."

"My God!" said Dr. Brown. He felt faint. "He would do that?"

"Who knows what goes on in that half-breed's head. Half the Indians won't have a thing to do with him on account of they think he's looney and the Mexicans don't want him neither. Though now, the Comanche seem to like him on account of he gave 'em the loot from a robbery down in Matamoros. Still it was one of them that pointed us this way.

"Listen, mister, we're talking about a man, here, who's twice as dangerous as your stock outlaw on account of he doesn't make any sense. Mexican Bill's no Jesse James. He's no respectable outlaw. He just gets mad and starts in on a town, whooping and hollering like a warrior on a raid and he shoots at anything that moves."

"I tole you it was Indians!" said Lemon.

"He said the man was Mexican, Lemon." Dr. Brown turned back to the marshal. "Marshal, you've got me very concerned now. This Mexican bandit might have taken Maybelleen for a ransom, perhaps? If that's the case, I'll pay it."

"I've been on his tail for some time now. This is how I see it. Mexican Bill? He's a man without a nation. He isn't American, isn't Mexican, and isn't Indian either. I figure that makes him all wobbledy headed. As far as killing goes, he's shot up a few. There's a story he shot a man in Kansas City for giving him a bad steak. So we can say he's mean-tempered.

"He rides with two old men, they rob banks and trains and shoot up towns. However, Mexican Bill is not only bad-tempered, he's stupid. In the past year his gang's only managed to get money out of one bank and that was because everyone ran away when they rode in because they thought it was the Hill Creek band.

"Those folks were twice as mad when they found out they'd been robbed by Mexican Bill. These men are just plain irritating and folks want 'em dead.

"Now my men here have been trailing this asshole for over a month and we're all dog tired. I'd like to go home to Denver and have a hot dinner but it looks like the imbecile has got your wife for some reason and that's enough to get any man riled up. Thing is, if they do got her then they'll be twice as easy to find. That is, if they haven't killed her. I doubt Bill'd have enough brains to try ransoming anything."

Dr. Brown pulled the Winchester from the saddle. "Marshal, I would like to ride with you and your men and find this Mexican Bill. If he's got my wife, then I'll be proud to shoot him straight through the heart."

"What are we gonna do then?" Shoe limped around the shack, smacking himself in the head. "We're as good as dead. You know those federal boys are right behind us, and they don't like you Bill, you've made 'em mad as snakes, doin' all this ridin' here and there. I say we leave her here and head straight up to Utah."

"We're not leaving her."

"I'm goin' home," said Vitus.

"Fine," said Shoe. "Less baggage."

"What about my opinion?" They all looked at Maybelleen, who had pulled herself up on her elbows. "I'm starving."

"Give her some jerky, Vitus," said Shoe.

"I don't have it, you have it."

"You feel better?" asked Mexican Bill.

"Yes," she said. "Who are you?"

"Let's just say we're Good Sammarians," said Bill.

"Sammarians?"

"Like on the road, the old man that was blind."

"The one that was raised from the dead," said Vitus.

"Lazarus? Oh," she said, "Samaritans."

"We got to get you to a doctor. Figure we'll get you over to Rain somehow," said Bill.

"Bill, I can smell them marshals and if'n we go one step east we're done for," said Shoe.

"So, I'm an impediment," said Maybelleen.

"Now you ain't no pediment," said Vitus, "anyone at all can see youse a lady."

Maybelleen threw back her head and laughed.

The three men looked at one another.

"I haven't laughed for a long time," she said. "Alright. Get me on a horse and let's head toward Rain. I gather that the three of you are outside of the law in some form or another but you've certainly been fine to me. I don't want to get in the way."

"You're not in the way," said Bill. "But we do have to leave before light. A few men are after us because we robbed a bank."

"Can't say we robbed it if'n we didn't get nothin'," said Shoe.

"We robbed it," said Bill, "and that's the final word."

"Robbin' to me means gettin' somethin' for the trouble," muttered Shoe.

"I'm feeling much better now and I can ride. Just point me toward Rain."

"There ain't no way you're ridin' alone," said Mexican

Bill, "after what you been through. We'll ride you there and then be off."

Shoe and Vitus looked at each other and back at Bill.

"Here we go," said Shoe, and Vitus nodded.

Maybelleen didn't feel that bad after all. Her head was banged up a bit and she was sore. The men had donated their old shirts from their bedrolls for bandages where she still bled off and on from a ragged cut by her eye.

The four rode east toward the town of Rain in a frozen drizzle. The sky was lightening as they saw the town about a mile in the distance.

Maybelleen looked at the man riding next to her.

"Bill" they'd called him. They were bank robbers, outlaws. Bill had black hair that flowed free nearly to his waist. His skin was dark and pitted and his nose was big enough to see from a long way away. He had a very definite chin.

He was the handsomest man she'd ever seen.

"We're just about there, ma'am," he said to her.

"You're very kind," she'd said back.

"Fact is, I'm not," he'd said, looking straight at her with black eyes. "Never have been except to a few strays. But I do have my honor, lady, and that ain't somethin' that can be placed lower on the line than life itself. So you just remember it, lady, when they say nobody can believe nothin' no more."

The other two men were riding behind them as they approached town. The rain had started to come down harder so when the first bullet flew by, Maybelleen thought it had started to hail.

"Hellfire, Bill! It's the Feds!"

"Damn, boys," said Mexican Bill, "load and fire and head for the rocks."

Maybelleen turned behind and saw what seemed to be a hundred men on horseback riding so fast she could see the water splashing up from the hooves of the horses.

"You stay right here, lady. They ain't gonna shoot at you," said Bill. "It's time for us to say good-bye."

And off they went, the three, toward a far mound of boulders.

Maybelleen sat there a moment on her horse, watching the men riding toward her and then at the men riding away.

"Maybelleen!" she heard, and there was Dr. Elias Brown, Winchester waving in the air. "Maybelleen, I'm coming!"

It was funny, she'd think later, how she'd suddenly seen everything happening around her in the strangest way. The sun had sneaked out from behind the heavy clouds and the rain had seemed to be made of diamonds. Through a million cold jewels, she'd seen her husband riding toward her and watched the stranger as he made for the rocks.

She'd known that guns were still firing for she'd heard the popping sounds. They'd sounded strangely like the beating of her heart. She'd sat there, the mare pulling her to the right, shifting its footing, as the men bore down toward her and then she watched as all but one pulled away like a single willed animal toward the big white boulders in the distance.

"Maybelleen!"

He'd been almost close enough to see into his eyes when she'd jerked the bridle with a rough hard hand and leaning down on her little mare's neck, she'd kicked its flanks and screamed *"Go!"*

She'd raced the horse and felt its bones between her legs, felt every muscle in its neck. It smelled of sea foam she'd thought. The sun caught the horse's every hair; the boulders in the distance sparkled. Still it rained. She rode on, leaning lower into the horse's neck. It seemed to know which way to go; the whipping mane blinded her and she melted into its body and sang, "Samarkand, Cairo, Phoenicia, Baghdad." She repeated this to the thud of hooves, like beads she ran the words through her lips. She felt every forward pull of the horse's legs as though she were running herself, stretched wide then bunched together, the legs exploding and eating distance. Through the crystalline veil of rain someone was yelling, "Stop firing, stop firing," but all she saw were the boulders ahead. Her foreign shore.

She made the rocks and found them there on the other side, lying down together on their bellies, guns pointing out at the riders who were just now at the base below.

They were very close. The men beneath them. A hundred feet perhaps, she'd realized.

"What now?" she'd said to Bill as she'd jumped down from her horse. Her heart pounded, her blood shrieked inside her. Her face was red, her eyes watering.

"Hell if I know," he'd said, and pulled her roughly down beside him.

"Alright Bill, let her go," someone had then yelled.

And they'd all looked at one another, the two old men staring at her like she was a ghost and Bill looking at her as if he had all the time in the world.

She'd smiled at him as she'd never, ever, smiled before.

"What the hell," he'd said and aimed his .44 through the rocks.

When he'd fired the sound had made her laugh. "Yes," she'd said out loud.

"You got the marshal," Shoe had said. "We're dead meat now."

"Aw, I winged him," said Bill. "He'll still eat dinner tonight."

"You goddamned, lowlife snake," screamed the marshal. "Let her go, you damned jumping bean, you lousy coward!"

Maybelleen heard the *ring ping* of bullets as they passed over her head and hit the rocks behind them.

"Stop firing, you idiots! There's a woman up there! Maybelleen, Maybelleen, it's Elias. You can come down now, dear."

Mexican Bill looked at Maybelleen. "Do you know him?" he said.

"Yes, I do, it's my husband."

"You wanna go down?"

"Isn't it amazing," she said to him then. She pointed past the rocks. A rainbow was forming very faintly in the air.

"Get going, lady," said Vitus, "this ain't no time for sightseein'."

"I know you're confused," she'd heard her husband shouting. "We're here to save you, dearest. Tell those men to let you go. Think clearly now, dear."

"I'm not coming, Dr. Brown," Maybelleen shouted back. "I'm not coming down. Not now, Dr. Brown, and not ever.

"Think of me as dead, Dr. Brown, and playing with the angels."

"Maybelleen!" and it seemed his voice was broken right in two. "What are you saying?"

"You're kinda hard on him," said Mexican Bill.

"Bill, you lousy bastard, I don't know what you've done to that woman, but you know you can't run with her. I've got a warrant for your arrest, but I'll give you a fair chance if you send the woman down now."

Bill rolled over on his back and looked at Maybelleen.

"That marshal's been followin' us for a month. He ain't

too fond of me. You do what you think's right, lady. I tole you before and I'll tell you again. I ain't one to go back on what I said. Some folks think the world's dead—"

"Bill!" A bullet hit a rock behind them and pieces of stone flew in Maybelleen's face. She blew the bits out of her mouth and wiped them away with the back of her hand.

"Don't shoot for God's sake, Marshal," said Dr. Brown, "my wife's unbalanced, but she'll see reason."

"But it's full of everythin' that was there before. It's all in how you see it," said Bill.

Maybelleen stood up behind the rocks and looked down on the men below. Her wet hair was plastered about her face. There was blood on her skirts. She lifted her fists and said, "Call me howling mad, Dr. Brown, tell them I'm just plain crazy."

The doctor jumped off his horse and started for the base of the rocks.

"Stop right there," she'd said. "Or I'll tell them to shoot you."

Dr. Brown had shaded his eyes. "Maybelleen—"

"Shut up. You're the marshal?" she said to the tall man in front. His forehead was bleeding where Bill's bullet had grazed him. "I suggest you and these men ride off right now and no one will get hurt. As I explained to my husband, Dr. Brown there, I have no intention of coming down from here."

"Ma'am," said the marshal, "I'm sure you know we aren't planning on shooting you, but perhaps you are unaware that the men you're with back there are wanted by the people of four states for robbery and murder.

"Now, I realize that you aren't in your right mind, your husband has explained that to me . . ."

As the marshal spoke Maybelleen signaled with her hand at the three men to move backward. Mexican Bill understood first and signed to Shoe and Vitus to get the horses. The rocks blocked them from view below.

". . . that you are confused. You've no doubt hit your head, you're not thinkin'."

"If I hit my head, Marshal, it woke me up." Maybelleen dropped back down and crawled behind the next barrier of rocks where Mexican Bill held her mare.

"Ready?" he asked.

"Ready," she said.

"Come on, lady," shouted the sheriff.

As they picked their way over the rocks to the other side she could faintly hear "Maybelleen, I'll take you home to Kentucky. You can sing and dance all you want, just please come down."

By the time the men realized that they were talking to no one at all, Maybelleen was already two miles away.

That was far enough to start over.

The marshal broke his leg in a barber shop in Red Rock, Arizona, and had to turn the search over to his second in command. Dr. Brown had been riding with them searching for Maybelleen but in Flagstaff he had a whiskey after a particularly empty day. Then he had a drink in Tucson and another in Santa Fe. After a month and a half of searching, looking here and looking there, he took a train from Kansas City back to Chicago. There he preached a new doctrine of Indian segregation.

And he drank at night. Sometimes he cried for an hour, remembering the smell of her elbow and the tissue softness of her neck. Sometimes he howled and cursed and threw things at the wall until there was nothing left to break.

But by then, she'd truly gotten far away. He knew he'd never, ever find her where she'd finally gone.

Margaret

Going On

Now here I am in snow.

Winter finds me no matter where I go. Jim was here for two hours today. He sat in the kitchen with the bright yellow cabinets. Aunt Opal told him stories and I saw him laugh. His teeth, though strong and white, are crooked, and I found myself thinking again about heredity and had to kick myself.

"I'm mostly Irish," he told Aunt Opal.

They were talking about where they came from.

"But American. That's what I am. I mean a bunch of us came over when there weren't any more potatoes, but that was a long time ago. American."

"I don't know if Margaret told you the Daniel Boone story," said Aunt Opal.

I was chopping red cabbage for coleslaw. Uncle Wendell loves coleslaw and it's the only way Aunt Opal can get him to eat a vegetable.

"He doesn't care about Daniel Boone," I said.

"Sure I do," Jim said.

"Another beer, Jim?" went Aunt Opal.

"I'm done with the cabbage," I said.

"Chop carrots," said Aunt Opal.

"I did."

"Chop some more. I'll make carrot-raisin salad."

"I think I'll go read awhile," I said.

"Get out those canned tomatoes, why don't you Margaret. There's some pickled okra and peaches. I need labels."

Aunt Opal is so easy to see through, I expect Jim to be embarrassed but he just says, "My ma used to can everything. I do miss that. I love pickled okra. She used to put in so much garlic it'd scare the law away."

"You are the law," I say, pulling the jars out of the cabinet.

"I wasn't then."

"Put aside four of them jars for Jim," says Aunt Opal. "Now. My mother was a MacGregor, Margaret's grandma Ivy was too. We were first cousins.

"The MacGregors come over here, this is how the story goes, our great-great-grandpa, that'd be Duncan MacGregor, was married to a Stewart who was descended directly from Queen Mary of Scotland, the one that got her head chopped off for trying to get the throne of England, so that's another side of the family tree. Anyway, Great-Great-Grandad, Duncan MacGregor, had a girl in about oh, 1720, sometime like that . . ."

"That's a funny thing," says Jim. "We had some Stewarts in our family, too. My ma told me her grandma was descended from the same Queen Mary too."

"I thought you were Irish," I said.

"I am."

"Queen Mary was a Scot," I say. I'm drawing pictures of tomatoes with faces on the labels.

"I guess I'm Scotch too," he says.

"Scottish. Scotch is whiskey," I say.

"As I was saying," says Aunt Opal.

"Right," says Jim.

"Don't you have to arrest anyone, the town drunk or someone? Or give out a parking ticket?" My tomato labels are pretty good, I think.

"It's my lunch break."

"Anyway," says Aunt Opal. "The girl, what would that be? A great-aunt, no, that's not right. She'd be . . ."

"Long lunch break," I say.

"She . . . now wait a minute here"—Aunt Opal's working on it, figuring it out on her hand.

"An aunt." I get up and stretch. I get a beer from the refrigerator.

"Honey," begins Aunt Opal.

"I stopped taking the pills," I say.

"I don't know that you should if the doctor says . . ."

"Aunt. She's right. It'd be an aunt," says Jim.

"Well. Pour me just a little glass, Margaret, just a tiny bit. I don't drink Jim, never do, well sherry on special occasions, but that beer you brought, last time I had a taste of beer was when I was a little thing and I found it so bitter. That's fine, honey. Oh! Goes right up your nose, doesn't it?" Aunt Opal burped and covered her face.

"I am so sorry. Excuse me. Indigestion. Must have been those peppers."

"A good burp is the sign of a clean engine, I was told," says Jim. "You were saying, Opal."

"Alright, now. This aunt, great as she was, married Daniel Boone when she was sixteen. He was old by then, we heard, and she had a baby by him, but if he wasn't already married to that other gal, Nancy, think it was, leaving our great-aunt stuck with a baby! That baby was another girl and somehow it never got recorded right in history.

"That's the Daniel Boone story. And it's true too. I know it because I heard it from my grandma. Ivy knew it too. Can you imagine? Daniel Boone was made into all kinds of a hero but he was a two-timer and a drunk. That's what I heard. Never know what kind of skeletons might be rattling away in the family press, do you?"

"Yep," I say. "Makes sense to me."

"I guess that's about it for me, then," says Jim. "No more than one at lunch." He tosses the beer can in the garbage. "Better hit the road."

"So good to know our arm of the law is right on top of things," I say. "Careful you don't drive the taxpayer's car right into a ditch."

But he ignores me and gives Aunt Opal a kiss on the cheek.

"Come by anytime," says Aunt Opal. "It's such a pleasure."

Jim puts on his thick green sheriff's jacket. It makes him look big. I give him the four jars and he juggles them for a minute then sticks one in each pocket, holding the other two in each hand.

"Margaret," he says.

I just look at him. We've had a few more dates and no matter how hard I try I can never pull away from those black eyes.

"Saturday there's a stock show over at Campbellsburg. It's a bit of a haul."

Aunt Opal concentrates on her little glass of beer.

"Cattle's what I'm looking at."

"Walk him to the door, Margaret," says Aunt Opal.

"I'll walk you to the door," I say.

Jim stands outside. Snow hits him right in the face. It hangs on his eyelashes and I stand back in the warm.

"I don't like farming," I say.

"Didn't say you did."

"I'm not interested in cows, either."

"Fine." He turns away and starts down the sidewalk. I begin to close the door as he slips and falls. The two jars of okra that he was holding go flying off in opposite directions and land in snow.

He looks at me, surprise all over his face, and then starts to laugh. I start laughing too and then his face changes, goes almost white.

"What's wrong? Are you hurt?" I run down the sidewalk to help him up and I see the other two jars have smashed inside his jacket.

We spend half an hour picking glass and okra from Jim's jacket. Aunt Opal has him take off his shirt too, and we pick some more from his naked sides. He's not hurt bad. Scarcely any glass got through the fabric. I paint the few places with Mercurochrome.

He looks so thin but his chest has a deep ridge between his breastbone. His arms are muscled from planting fence posts and putting down fertilizer.

How we end up at the farm I really can't say.

We went to the stock show and the smell of manure filled the arena and took me back to my childhood. It's a hot fertile smell and I'd forgotten how much I used to take it for granted. It was one of those smells that went along with everything else, and taken away, just that one smell, the whole world didn't smell quite right.

But now, sitting up in the graveyard, the sun orange, just above the naked black trees and that smell gone away I'm in pieces again.

I said to Jim after the show, after hotdogs and beer, let's just drive. Let's just drive. And we ended up here.

"Pretty land," he said, sitting on the hill, looking down at the little lake. "I can't believe you just wanna let it lie here."

"Well I do," I say, throwing a rock at the frozen lake.

"Cold?"

"Not really," I say.

I showed him Maybelleen's grave and all he said was, "Hum, that's interestin'."

"Don't you know who she was?" I asked him, while he smoked another cigarette.

"Sure, I heard of her. What's in the lake?"

"Jesus, Jim. I can't believe you. Maybelleen MacGregor was probably the greatest living woman outlaw in this country, in the whole United States. Do you know what she stood for?"

"Nope." He goes on smoking, looking down at his cigarette like it's the fountain of all knowledge.

"For freedom! For . . . she suffered, Jim. She was a hero, a martyr. Do you know she was convicted and nobody ever proved that she even ever killed anyone? Do you realize they hung her for being nothing less than just a woman who decided to take life in her own hands and . . ."

Then he kissed me. He just grabbed me by the back of the neck and hauled me over to him and kissed my lips.

"She was a queen!" I try to say but he's pried open my mouth with his tongue.

"You're a queen," he said.

In the snow. In the snow, in the graveyard, we made love. Right there in front of her. We just melted everything around us. And myself, I felt something. Like something woke up and even at the end, in the dismal business of fastening everything and wiping things off, I wasn't ashamed or embarrassed or even anything but mixed up and I was shaking my head, I just couldn't stop it.

Then he grabbed me and kissed me again, long and hot enough to make me dizzy and set everything into a spin.

"So what's in the lake," he says then, tucking in his shirt and reaching down for my hand.

"Sunfish. Striped bass," I say.

We smoked cigarettes and the sun went down and then we both started shivering.

Here I am again, home. Wrapped up in the peach bedspread. Shivering still. But not from cold.

I raise my hands to the dark ceiling.

I do need a sign.

Maybelleen
1901

With Bill

The sky has always been blue. That's what she thought as she unrolled her blanket and curled up next to Bill. Behind the clouds the color never changed.

It's all how you see it. That's what she thought.

They'd finally hit Judgment after waiting a week. The Indians had hidden them deep in a cave. The marshals had searched every house on the reservation. No one but the Comanches knew about the cave.

Then, when the law thought they'd headed up to the Dakotas, they'd gone on to hit Cross Land, Arizona. Got the Miner's Bank without shooting a fly. They rode fast and by ways that only Bill knew about. Down in Texas, folks in Jesusville and Crowbar started laughing at the Rangers, after they robbed the banks there in the blink of an eye.

A half-breed, a cripple, and an old Negro were robbing everything in sight. Folks had heard it was all planned by a schoolmarm.

Since she'd joined them they always made off with the money, and now they were rich and more wanted and the sky was blue.

Loving Bill was every foreign destination she'd ever imagined.

They were wanted by four states. Maybelleen's picture had been in the *Lexington Ledger* and the *Louisville Journal*. They'd drawn her with two six-shooters blazing and a crazy-eyed Indian riding right behind her.

So they lived mostly in dry creek beds and caves and on Indian land. And always they kept moving ahead of the law.

Maybelleen MacGregor felt finally alive.

The sky has always been blue, she thought, turning to Bill in the rain. I just couldn't see it.

She kissed him and they laughed as the water fell on them. She kissed the tiny rivers that ran down his face.

In Cutler, in the Territory, she'd showed her stuff to them all.

Vitus had threatened once again to leave. Shoe had snorted.

Bill showed her how to shoot while they camped in the brush.

He'd given her a pretty .32, a Smith & Wesson. The feel of it in her hand made her see things a new way.

She said, "There's one life and only one way to live it. I'll live it no matter what the consequences might be."

No one was hurt in Cutler and it all went smooth as silk.

They'd hit the bank at three-thirty, right before it closed. She'd gone in first with the widow story. She needed to bank her dead husband's dollars.

And she looked so respectable, like a lady and all.

They'd been moving so quick, first Kansas, then Texas. Although it was shrinking, the West was still a place where if you rode fast you beat the telegraph, the trains, and the mail.

First she'd done the planning, letting Bill make his speeches. About Indian rights and saving money for his Wakan Tanka visions. Shoe and Vitus would grumble, as they always did. But now they knew they'd get a share when before they'd got nothing.

"And this is it, ya ol' coot," Shoe would say to Vitus when he went on about his rheumatism, "it's the wild ride that matters."

Maybelleen was just what they'd needed. She leveled Bill's crazy head out, he would listen to her. His Indian dreams grew grander but May planned the robberies. She used psychology and the simplest logic. They had a backup plan and used their heads instead of doing it raw. It wasn't outlawing the way they'd done it before.

Instead of just riding into a town with sixteen different

notions, they began to hit with a solid and well-rehearsed plan.

It worked. It was simple. Why hadn't they done it before?

It was like Maybelleen was the focus that Bill had been missing. "It's clear to me now," he'd tell them all, "what life is and what love is. You got to work to get there and that goes for it all. Are we outlaws? I imagine we got to be better then than most. If we're outlaws we got a responsibility here. Can't just take money, got to do somethin' with it. Got to make somethin', build somethin'. Leave somethin' behind."

It had always seemed to Shoe and Vitus that Bill was mad as a hatter. And his Indian schemes grew ever more vast and grander until he was talking of taking all of Mexico over. But Bill had always been singular. That's why they loved him, and with Maybelleen along, they began to believe the whole thing themselves.

They were past fifty, both Shoe and Vitus. They had seen things pass away right in front of their eyes. They both rode with Bill because their world was ending and at least with Bill they felt it wasn't all over yet. A last stab at things the way they used to be, because it was changing at a speed that plain scrambled their minds.

In Santa Fe they watched tourists buy baskets from Indians, drink champagne, and take photographs of picturesque pueblos. In Albuquerque folks went to hear an opera at night. Kansas City had proper restaurants, sidewalks, and circuses. Tombstone was already a stop on the tourist train.

Their world was circling ever smaller and smaller. Neither of them wanted to die in a bed.

But Maybelleen and Bill would dance out in the moonlight. In the desert where no one else could find them. Shoe and Vitus would sing songs that already were forgotten. Bill and Maybelleen had a spirit that was dying all around.

Out in the desert, Shoe began talking of buying cattle below the Rio Grande. Away from the new West and out under the stars, Shoe talked of putting together a herd that would put Texas to shame. Vitus said he'd prospect the mountains of Vera Cruz and find diamonds and rubies and lost Spanish treasure. When they got to Mexico, they'd have the world at their feet. Bill with his Indians and Maybelleen. Maybelleen with her Bill. They'd all live together with the law to themselves.

Now Maybelleen wanted to be in on the action. She craved it and wanted to be right beside Bill. She wanted to hear him say, "This is a holdup and don't nobody move."

Maybe she thought it would be like in books, like the legends she'd read over and over in Kentucky. Bill was a good man, outside of the law, and therefore there was nothing they could do that was wrong. She turned the idea around in her mind.

You have to question things, she said to herself. Sometimes you have to do something wrong to get it right.

Bill did it for the Indians. Maybelleen did it for love. Shoe and Vitus did it because they had nothing to lose.

So in Cutler, Maybelleen kept the bank manager busy.

"I might want to put in more," she'd said, counting out hundreds. From the front of the bank, Bill then told the tellers, "This is a holdup."

May looked at the manager and said, "Nobody move."

When the manager stood, Maybelleen had pulled out her gun. Sweetly she'd asked him to sit or get shot full of holes.

Vitus had locked the front door when he'd come in. Pulled down the shades so no one outside thought a thing. The bank was closed as was normal. They left everyone tied up and exited calmly.

Maybelleen left town first, occasioning some comment. A lone woman rider was a bit unusual. But no one really paid it much attention. Cutler was a boomtown, they had other things to do.

Bill and Shoe had a drink at Miller's Saloon. Vitus bought two loaves of fresh baked bread. He was always hungry.

They were thirty miles away by the time the robbery was discovered and they rode fifteen more and spent that night in Honey Grove, a town already past booming. No one thought to look for them there.

Bill and Maybelleen danced all that night until the sun came up and then they slept all the next day.

All during this time she never thought of Dr. Brown. She never thought of Kentucky except as a flash once in a while. All her life had been spent trying hard to find something. Once it was found, nothing else existed.

The time with Bill became the sum of her life.

At night she told stories, kept Shoe begging to hear more of "Frankenstein" and "The Pit and the Pendulum," which she knew almost by heart. What she didn't remember, she made up. She did it so well that in the firelight the old man's face dropped away years.

"How do I dare, Mrs. Reed? Do you think I have no feelings? I remember how you pushed me into the red room and locked me up all the day and night. I was in agony and alone and so afraid. Do you think I can live without love and tenderness?"

And Shoe would blow his nose loudly into his overcoat for the poor little orphan, Jane Eyre.

She practiced shooting her gun, firing at tumbleweed and cactus.

She shot a snake that had curled up in her boot.

She dreamed of buffalo from the first time she'd made love to Bill.

Five months were a minute. Six months were a hundred years.

After eight months, she'd sometimes sit outside alone and then she'd remember things sometimes, remember her mother, her sister. She'd even feel sorry for Dr. Brown. She'd look all around at the foreign things; the castle clouds, the way smoke rose differently in outside air. She saw that cactus were trees in a different landscape. She watched bats swoop in watercolor air and realized they were the most graceful of all night birds. And she wished that she could have a child with Bill.

Because that would be something more real than anything. That would be something to always hold on to.

She rode with Bill to Taos to see the Indians there. He gave them three thousand dollars and told them he was buying land down in Mexico where all Indians could live free.

Most laughed at him but took his money. Most thought he was crazy.

"Don't sell your honor," he'd tell them. "Not the things that you've made. Come to Mexico."

"What tribe are you," they'd ask him. "You're not one of us. The whites buy our pottery, our necklaces too. What do you know about it? You're an outlaw, we thank you. The money is good. But you're not one of us. Don't come and tell us what to do."

What tribe was he? Maybelleen never knew. One day he was Blackfoot and one day Sans Arc.

"I'm Sioux," Bill had told her.

And this month he was Paiute and tonight he'd been Crow.

And that's when she knew that he didn't have a clue where he came from. As far as bloodlines were concerned he only knew he was half Indian. The Mexican part came from his father because the nuns had told him that.

He'd been raised until eleven in the convent of La Reina de las Palmas in Texas. He had a last name, he'd told her, but he'd forgotten it now.

After they'd hit Jesusville, when they were lying on their stomachs in a rented room in the Territory, he told her about the time he'd visited his grandmother.

"She came and got me," he told her.

"My little grandmother died right there at Wounded Knee. She was shot in the back by the soldiers. But when I was little, my grandmother came down to Texas and got me and took me back to Pine Ridge. For three months I was happy and I lived as a Sioux. My people had been shamed, had been beaten but never had they been broken in two.

"Then the missionaries came and got me and took me back to Texas. And I found out later that they killed her and Sitting Bull, too."

"I knew Sitting Bull at Standing Rock," he told her another time. "I was there when they trapped him, when the Fort Yates soldiers came and shot him up and murdered him. They filled him full of holes and left him to die like a dog."

"Then we'll go back there," she told him. "We'll see your people again."

"Can't go back," he told her.

Had he been there at all? She didn't know, didn't care.

But he knew all the stories. He knew how to find places in

the dark, he could live in mountains and even in dry grass. He found food in the desert and steered by the stars. Everywhere they went, all the Indians knew him. But he never seemed to find the ones he was searching for.

"These aren't my people," he'd tell her. "But they're my brothers, nonetheless. We're all the same tribe, anyway, no matter what the whites say."

"I thought they were at Pine Ridge," Maybelleen would say.

"Maybe they're dead," Bill would answer. "I haven't found them at all."

And Bill never lied. Bill told the truth in the way that he saw it. He was the most honest man she'd ever known.

At Crow Creek Reservation Bill went in at night and met with the men in an unpainted clapboard house to tell them his great plan.

Maybelleen sat quiet in the back of the room while Bill told them of his vision.

When he was finished speaking an old man stood up and said, "This man is a brother to us. We know Bill. He's been here before and he's never lied.

"We won't take your money because it does us no good. You keep it, Bill, and you keep that vision. I, for one, am honored that you have shared it with us.

"The white man has chopped us in a thousand pieces like a snake. He's scattered us from here to there. But he never noticed that the pieces are still moving. You see that and that's a vision that you and I share.

"Many have given up, times have hurt us and killed many among us. It seems we live in shadows of what we once were. None of the young ones have ever seen a buffalo and my son even asks me why I bother to tell stories. He's been schooled by the whites and lives on a farm. Laughing Crow, my daughter, wears lace and ribbons and is married to the rancher from Moon River Lake. We are scattered and taught not to remember.

"But see him? Come here, boy. Come here to my knee."

Maybelleen watched as a little boy, about four years old, came to the old man. The boy smiled and stood between the old man's legs.

"This is Passing Hail, my grandson. They call him Willy. He knows the stories and that's my revenge.

"I've told him someday there will be a new place for the People. It is promised by my vision and it will be. I tell them all that. But I don't think that it's here on the ground where we are sitting. We've been trapped here in this place. I think it's in the sky. But maybe this is the place you speak of, that I can't say."

The old man sat down.

"We'll take the money, Bill," said a young man. "Six Horses is old. We and my Lakota brothers will take the money to buy guns. There ain't no other place for us but what we take back. We ain't waiting around for a place in the sky."

"Be quiet, John Gunn," said Six Horses. "You're a fool and will be hung in not much more time. You steal horses and cattle and the whites will hang you for that."

John Gunn spat on the ground. "I take old ones that might die and they don't know if they did. I'm not stupid but I'm tired of living like a dog. What's the worth of anything if we let the government just take and take from us? You want to lay down and die?

"All you old men do is talk about a beautiful land in the sky. We won't wait, old man."

Bill had stood between them. "Brothers, for you are my brothers. I have nobody else.

"I am Indian, but maybe from a hundred tribes. I promise you I will buy a place to go to, with water running through it and grassland and no fences. And no American government to drag us from here to there."

"Mexico has no government, then?" asked John Gunn. "Mexico will take us in and shelter us and let us be free?" He spat on the ground. "Brothers, who the hell do you think you are?

"You're a fool, Mexican Bill, you'll be hanging soon, too. We don't want your Mexico, we want our own land. The land of our fathers. And if we die getting it, then so much the better."

"Maybe," he said. "That's probably true. If they catch me they'll hang me but at least I believe. And Mexico has a government, sure. But I'm buying so much land that they'll have to leave us alone and when all the tribes send their people, it'll be a new force to reckon with. Then we can get back the old land again."

"Dreams," said John Gunn. "Buy guns not dreams. You're no tribe at all. You don't know where you come from, you know nothing at all."

The men rose up to follow John Gunn out of the house. None looked at Bill.

Maybelleen watched Bill then as he picked up the money. He'd laid it all out as a sign of his good intentions. He moved slow and deliberate. She couldn't read his face. But she knew that the pain he felt was greater than any stab wound and she rose to go to him when Six Horses spoke.

"The time's gone, Bill. It's gone for the great gathering of the tribes. We had the world for a thousand seasons and we treated it like a precious child. That was the thing we did and we know we did it right. But somewhere something happened, who can say what the Great Spirit dreams? Who can say who is the dreamer and who is the dream?

"But dreams are power, Bill, if you follow their trail. I can't tell you not to do this, because it's only your path.

"You heard what they say. You might find some to follow

you. But do you think the government's going to just let them walk away?"

"Why, they're not prisoners," said Bill.

"Oh, yes they are," said Six Horses. "They're prisoners not just of the whites, but also of their fear. They've grown afraid and so will kill themselves to kill that same fear. They buy guns but know that by doing so, they kill themselves. We all know that the white man wants us all dead. They only hope to die with the dignity of warriors.

"But go ahead, Bill. You buy this land and I'll send down my grandson. If you can make this place, I will send him to you.

"That I promise."

But Bill never could understand why most Indians wouldn't see it. Still, it never kept him from trying. For he'd had the vision. May's buffalo dream. His vision.

Once, he went away for two days and left her in a little North Dakota mining town.

When he returned, she didn't hear him, she'd been looking out the window, wondering where he had gone.

He'd pulled her down upon the brass bed and said, "Everything has a reason, May."

But it didn't matter one way or another because in three months he'd be dead.

At Chandler, the real problems had begun and most had to do with Young Pup.

Stuart Ray Colvin had joined them in Crowbar. He'd rode out of town with them as though he'd been part of the gang. So intent were they on getting away that it wasn't until they were a mile out that anyone noticed him.

"What the hell," said Vitus. And he'd drawn his gun. He would've fired if Maybelleen hadn't shouted, "Wait!"

She'd quickly seen that he was just a boy and nervous and sweating.

"What you want?" Bill had asked as they ringed around him on their horses.

"Just to ride with you," he'd said and then he'd said, "Please?"

"Kill 'im, Vitus," Shoe had said. "He's after the bounty that's what."

"No, I ain't," said the boy, "I'm lookin' for a gang. I tried to get up my own but there's no one to be had. They worship too much and don't take life serious."

Bill had gotten down off his horse and the men dragged the boy off of his.

"Why," Bill had said, "do you want to ride with us?"

"Why I heard of you!" said the boy. "You're Mexican Bill and that's Maybelleen. It's all that I've wanted since I first saw your names on the posters in town. I knew you was serious and I can shoot."

"We ain't shooters," Bill had said. "Now get goin'."

"Please, mister," he'd said. "I'm as good as dead. I shot a man in town, who was tryin' to put together a posse."

"What posse?" Bill had said. "We just robbed the damn bank twenty minutes ago. Ain't no town can put together a posse that quick."

"Well, he said he was going to. So I shot him in the head."

"We don't want a kid," said Vitus, "especially a killer."

"He ain't dead," said the boy. "I just winged 'im."

"Well, we can't sit here talking about it," Maybelleen put in. "We've got twenty-five miles to ride tonight. Let him come."

"What is this?" said Vitus. "Who're you to give orders?"

"This is stupid," said Shoe. "He's just a pup, is all."

They'd mounted their horses and Maybelleen had smiled. There was something in the boy's face that she recognized from seeing herself.

"You want 'im?" Bill had asked her.

And Stuart Ray Colvin became part of the gang.

That's when it all started coming apart.

Two weeks later she'd noticed how he'd been when they'd gone back to the reservation late at night to meet with the Pawnees.

The boy had said later, before they'd all bedded down, "What's he want with these stinkin' Indians anyway? They all hate him, that's plain to see. Where's all the gold he's been robbin'? Ain't you all rich?"

"It's for the land in Mexico," said Shoe. "Now shut up and go to sleep."

"Mexico," said the boy. "That's dumb. We oughta spend it, that's what."

"Hush," Maybelleen had said then. "Or he'll wake up and hear you. He might just kill you for talking like that."

"I ain't skeered of Bill, May. He's crazy, don't you see?"

"Hush, Pup," she'd said. "Go to sleep."

He had a way of lookin' at Bill after learning that Bill gave most of the money he robbed to the Indians. And he watched Maybelleen strange when she spoke or walked.

"How much ya got, Vitus," she'd heard him ask once. "Twenty thousand, what? Ya really gonna let him take it to Mexico?"

Vitus had looked at him and never said a word.

"Where are you from, Pup?" she'd asked one night, when he'd been staring hard at her for about an hour.

"From Crowbar? Did you leave your parents back there?"

"Nope," he'd said. "Don't have no one. My ma died when I was twelve. Had an aunt but she died on me too. I was in Crowbar, lookin' to get some ranchin' work. You got pretty eyes, May," he'd said.

"Thank you, Pup," she'd said. "Please keep your hands to yourself, honey."

He'd pulled back his hand from her face like she'd burned him.

He was a tall brooding boy. Shoe and Vitus made fun of him. "Pup, ya dumb mutt" is what Shoe called him.

"What's wrong with your face, kid," Vitus would say, "whatcha got growin' there?"

"Leave him alone, boys. He's got dimples, is all," May would say, as they'd all sat bored in a small town, waiting for things to blow the other way. Bill would whittle sticks into strange shapes and tell Indian stories.

There was time like that. Plenty of it. They had to be careful, they were recognized now.

Before Stuart Ray Colvin had joined them, Bill and May had spent hours singing. Once they'd waltzed on a mesa top as Maybelleen had hummed "The Blue Danube."

Bill, Shoe, and Vitus had told stories for hours and Maybelleen had told them the history of the world.

But now, Pup, as they called him, always interrupted with "Aw, who cares," or, "I thought you was outlaws, but you're nothin' but crazy."

"Ride away," Bill would say and the others would laugh.

"We were all eighteen before, Bill."

And Maybelleen would smile at the boy. He'd stare and stare at her with those great, sad eyes.

Then Maybelleen would kiss Bill. She didn't see the fist that the boy made. The way he slammed it into his knee.

Vitus and Shoe told Bill to get rid of him. "He's no good, Bill," they'd told him. "He's rotten to the core."

"He's a kid," Bill would say and forget all about it.

Once when Bill was away for two days, the boy had come up behind her while she did laundry in a rocky, rushing stream.

"Why do you love that half-breed?" he'd asked her, his arms around her waist.

"For heaven's sake, Pup!" she'd said then. She'd pushed him away. "That's enough. I'm old enough to be your mother."

"No, you ain't." He'd walked away then, through the scrub oak and back to the camp.

Two hours later, Shoe and Vitus left to hunt rabbit and Maybelleen was lying down by the fire. She had Bill's *Walden* and was flipping through it.

"Can you read, Pup?" she'd asked him and he hadn't said a thing, but he'd come over and pushed her hard, back on the ground.

He'd put one hand on her right breast and brought his knee up between her legs. Then he'd come down upon her neck with his lips and covered her with wet kisses.

"I love you, I love you."

That's what he'd said. She'd pushed him and they'd rolled together until she'd smacked him across the face.

"If you ever again touch me, I'll kill you," she'd said. "And you're a fine-looking boy. But I'm Bill's woman and I'm crazy and don't you forget it. I'd have no trouble shooting you, right between the eyes."

"Aw, May," he'd said then. But that had been all.

She'd said nothing to Bill, nor Vitus or Shoe. She'd treated the boy the same as always.

But he only got worse.

When he'd look at Bill, she could see that there was murder in his eyes. And she realized that this boy wasn't right at all.

She'd thought he was a dreamer, that's why she'd taken him along. To ride with the rest of them as they dreamed out their lives. But he wasn't a dreamer.

He was far more real. He was incapable of dreaming. He saw only in white, in black. Maybelleen tried to understand him, to teach him about all the shades of gray layered in between in the world. But he didn't listen. He didn't care and he couldn't see them anyway.

So one night while he slept, before they hit the next town, she told Bill he'd have to tell him that the next job would be his last.

"He's trigger-happy and young. That's a normal thing."

Bill never noticed anything but her anymore. He was blind to the things around him, except his dream in his head. "Maybelleen, I love you." That's what he said. "But sure, we'll leave him behind if that's what you want. Now come here, you wiggling fish, and tell me a story."

But the next job was the last and then Bill was dead.

＿ﾙﾙ◎

In the cities and towns from Boston to Waco, Maybelleen MacGregor's name was on thousands of lips.

Why, she'd left her preacher husband to ride with an outlaw. She flaunted her adultery in the face of them all. She was a murderess, an adulteress and worse. She killed this one and that one just for blinking an eye. That's what they heard. It was scandalous, for sure.

But Maybelleen never killed anyone at all. She shot wildly in Chandler, when they'd trapped Bill all around, as he'd lain there getting shot she'd fired her gun. But no one was killed, she was too scared to aim.

While Pup was sitting back at the hideout. That's what had happened. Bill got shot nearly dead while the kid sat up in the cabin.

It began the same way all their robberies had begun. With careful planning and laughter and the dream they believed. By now, all Vitus and Shoe ever dreamed of was Mexico because they were old and never wanted to kill anyone anyway.

This was the last one and they would be on their way. Over the border to begin the dream.

In the back of their minds, the old men were different. They knew they might die each time they rode into a new town. Maybelleen and Bill never thought about dying. But this day they all felt good.

Even the kid had been smiling as they laid out the plan. The big one, the last one. This was it.

They'd surveyed the town two days before. They knew which way in and they knew three ways out. The bank was on the outskirts, the one they were robbing. It was perfect, it was glorious.

Later in the bank, Maybelleen would recall, how it'd all seemed so unreal the way everything began to unravel. Like a string pulled from a tapestry. The whole picture came apart a thread at a time.

At first it was wonderful. Everyone smiling. Bill and Maybelleen and their victims all seemed satisfied enough.

Those being robbed and those robbing seemed to have an explicit understanding. Even the mayor, who'd been making a deposit, had given a nice little speech.

"We're being robbed, fellow citizens, by Mexican Bill. We all know the reputation of these folks. Now let's all just cooperate and get this thing over. I've got a wedding at sundown I've got to get to."

"That's nice, Mayor," Bill had said as he'd clapped him on the back, "but how do you know us? We've got masks on, and anyway, we've never been your way before."

"Bill, we all know you by that long, flowing hair and Maybelleen there is the only female outlaw I've heard of in years. We all know your lady fair's reputation for killin' anything that moves, so we'll cooperate nicely here. Just don't shoot us, please, and we're honored to be robbed by the best."

"Thank you," said Maybelleen. "We're trying hard to get better."

"And we don't kill people, unless they try to kill us," added Mexican Bill. "We rob, see, to help others that the white man's forgot. It ain't a typical selfish thing. I always try to make that point clear."

But just then the bank manager reached for a handkerchief. His nose was running because he was scared out of his wits. He was the only one not honored at all. He was afraid of losing his bank and his allergies went wild. He sneezed once and reached for his green pocket silk.

And then Young Pup blew him to heaven.

In the space of a sneeze Maybelleen's months compressed to a single moment.

The double-gauge shotgun had scattered the man's brains on the walls and left only an eye and half a nose on his face.

There had been screaming then, ladies being present at the bank, and suddenly there were guns going off everywhere.

Maybelleen had frozen to the earth and Vitus or Shoe shot the mayor as he drew.

No one saw Pup as he ran through the door because the teller had a Remington propped up on the counter and was firing wildly, taking chunks out of the wall and splattering plaster.

Shoe and Vitus got out the door next and Maybelleen had just stood there, as Bill ran out the back way and into the waiting guns.

Why, they'd known they were coming and how could they know?

Maybelleen ran as fast as she could, around the corner where Shoe and Vitus sat waiting on their horses, and they'd ridden to Bill but he was trapped behind the bank.

Maybelleen had dropped down and fired all around from behind a wood fence. She'd fired and never remembered firing and reloading.

But by then Bill had taken at least fifteen rounds.

Vitus had ducked under the peeled wood fence. Forever she'd see every knot in that wood.

He'd dragged Bill away, how they'd missed him was a miracle. But everything she'd ever known with Bill had been miraculous.

She hadn't noticed that the boy was nowhere around. They'd ridden away with their lives. And Bill losing his.

But he'd turned back up. Like he'd been there all along, trailing like a ghost behind them. Staring at her through the night as Bill died. Standing apart as Bill was rolled into the grave.

She had a faint memory after Bill died, of Shoe and Vitus beating the boy, and she'd been going to say something but it had gotten lost in her mind.

"If it weren't fer you, gettin' panicked and startin' off shootin', we'd all be ridin' with Bill down to Mexico, ya cowardly little shit."

Then Shoe and Vitus ran away.

That's what he'd said. And she'd pretended to believe it.

Bill dead. Buried maybe four feet deep in loose desert dirt. Any coyote could have ripped that cheap soil away like skin from bones.

Maybelleen sat and listened to everything around.

Did it matter that she had it? What everyone says they want. True love. For a moment, a split second and even something less than that in the eye blink of time.

Now here she was in a town called Mud, or Mud Town. She didn't even know. People held their babies to her little cell window to show them the outlaw.

She ignored them. At least she told herself she did.

Hanging wouldn't matter and the sooner the better. Locked up here in the jail with feeling tingling from her bones to the tips of her toenails—now, that was far worse than any death devised.

And of course Shoe and Vitus would never run away.

The boy had killed them dead.

And Bill too. And left her.

Love.

She'd seen Bill and it had smacked into her, this love, right deep in her chest. She'd understood the whole universe.

But she couldn't love the boy and it somehow turned in on him. Love twisted around inside him and got caught on his heart. Now what is that, she wondered. And she caught herself trying and trying to understand. As though it were an incredibly difficult mathematical problem; how many barleycorns placed end to end would it take to circle the equator? How big is a barleycorn? Perhaps the equator shifted and changed as ice melted or formed at the faraway poles.

In two more days it will all be over, she thought.

But she knew how time could be encapsulated. She understood how time could be caught; slowed and worried to death. Just as easily as it could slip under a door and be gone.

Fourteen thousand sunrises, one hundred thousand memories and everything to know and see. In two longest, quickest days.

It wasn't easy.

Margaret

The Difference

I've done it.

I've found it.

The box in the back of the closet where Aunt Opal hid it. The box, I have it, right here on the bed.

I've got the lights on, both, one on each side, so the light can fall down on what it is that's inside.

I open the lid and see all the papers, there's a picture, it's my grandmother when she was young.

She was so beautiful, my grandmother, with long golden hair and lips that are smiling.

And here she is. Maybelleen.

I never saw this one before. Staring straight at the camera.

She's not pretty at all. There's a harshness to her features, too angular, too sharp. Her eyes draw me in, they hold something deep.

What's she thinking, I wonder and I turn over the photo. It was taken out west and the edges are worn.

Next to her is a man, must be the preacher, I figure. His face is heavy with whiskers and such a serious face. It says 1899.

Next, in an envelope, this must be her hand, is a letter addressed to my grandmother and I pull it out and tear the edge.

"Oh," I say out loud. Because I've torn it, it's like tissue, this paper. The tear rips right down and cuts into the page.

Dearest Ivy;

No doubt you've heard all the worst.

I'm writing this letter to let you know that I love you and I hope that you will not think too badly of me in the end.

Ivy, I did it. I did what I wanted. But I never killed anyone. At least, I never shot them. But these people want only to believe what they've made up their minds to.

I met a man, Ivy, and it was like something I was supposed to do all along. From the moment we're born, I think we have something to do with our lives. Back home I used to sit there and daydream, as you will remember, about cities and countries to which I'd never go. I never meant to hurt anyone, least of all you or Mama. But now Mama is dead, that's what they've told me. Somehow, I think that Mama might have understood this more than you will and no, I'm not crazy.

Ivy, I hope that your life will be as filled with love as mine was. Even though it was a short love it filled my entire life. We didn't rob banks or people just for the money, we had nowhere to spend it in any event. When you're running from the law, it isn't as if you can go shopping. As a matter of fact, I'll be hanged in a donated dress. I robbed banks with a man who had a beautiful vision. He believed in something and he did what he could to make it true.

The man I loved they called a killer. He was, I guess. He did shoot people and they died and I don't mean to sound coldhearted. Bill never got any satisfaction out of killing at all. So to me, he never was really a killer at all. Now I know what you're thinking, this all sounds quite mad. But sometimes you realize that you have to question things. Bill questioned and questioned and couldn't find any good answers so he went out and made an answer himself. He had a dream, and a good one, even if it was a bit naive. It came from the right place and he honored his dream. That's more than most people do.

The strange thing is, Bill never knew who he really was. But it never stopped him or slowed him down. Because to Bill it wasn't heredity that mattered in the end. What mattered was what you believed was right.

I can't say that we went about things in a correct manner. I've thought about it and it seemed that the whole time I was with him was a dream. It went by so fast and I got caught and began to dream too. The law is the law and we broke it. I'm not afraid of dying and I know there's something else out there, not heaven as we think of it but something after all. Maybe just by going back to where we began is the most beautiful heaven of all. I think Bill's somewhere where his native people are, I only hope that I can get there and they'll let me come.

I have no regrets. I believe I was right for me. I'm sorry for you that there's a reputation involved. Yours.

Dr. Brown has written me. I believe he's in Chicago. His letters are wild and have such a loneliness. He blames me, of course, for hurting him or "killing him" as he puts it. I am even responsible for his disengagement with the Lord. I don't know, Ivy, I turn this all around in my mind. I have, believe me, haunted hours in this place. There's nowhere to go to in this little room and I can't even see the setting sun. Oh, to be locked in a room with your memories sitting about you, I can't tell you. I was wrong, though. I'm sorry for Dr. Brown. I married him and pledged to love him when I didn't at all. I blamed him for my miseries and only realized my vanity when I finally found what love truly means. Love cannot be forced. And all living things love. Even a boy who loved me once, I think, will come to know that someday.

Next week they will hang me. I'm sure that you know that. I've never seen such a swarm of reporters!

Now, don't you worry about me, they were going to hang me right or wrong, anyway. There's nothing any of us can do about that now.

Ivy, life's short. I hope you do what you want to. It doesn't mean that you have to ride off to the West. I mean that you have to find your heart's desire and love it and live it and then say, I've had the best.

I love you always,
Maybelleen

Her words. I smooth out the tissue again on the bed. Her words float inside me like a healing hand.

Inside the box is another envelope. I open it and keep staring at the strange written words. I read them fine, in

English, of course. There they are. But no, they float in front of my eyes as though in Chaldaen or the hieroglyphs of some time I've completely forgotten.

I can't really read them, I'm not sure what they say.

But I can.

That's it. No matter how it's written. I read and know that it's completely true and even if it were revealed to me in a cave painting in France, I would know.

"When did she leave?" he asks and Aunt Opal is shaking her head.

"I don't know exactly, Jim. Wendell says the truck's gone.

"Oh, they should have told her all those years back!" She blows her nose again and her eyes are so puffy she can't close them. She paces back and forth in the peach-colored room.

He looks down at the paper he holds in his hand.

Sees the picture of Maybelleen lying on the bed.

"I hid these things from her because that's what Ivy wanted. She wasn't ever supposed to know."

"God," he says. He reads it again.

Mason County, Kentucky, it says. Certificate of Adoption.

"Ivy never told them they were adopted, both of those children. She couldn't could she, when her daughter died and there was no one left? She and Sam adopted them after her daughter died in an accident. Right off the train they brought those babies all the way from an orphanage out east. They never knew who their parents were. They didn't care, don't you see! They meant well, they did! They loved them like their own! And Ivy was like to go mad, after Maybelleen died and then her own girl. It was the best thing could've happened, them taking them kids. But I knew it was bad when that child began sniffing out Maybelleen. It was like she was always just hunting for something."

"No kin at all," says Jim, looking again at the paper.

"No, none," says Aunt Opal, wiping her face.

"I told Wendell we should tell her, I just had a feeling. Look at this. Look at how things happen!"

Jim turns away, the paper still in his hand. "I'll find her," he says.

He drives his green truck faster than he's ever driven before. The farm is at least a half hour away. He pushes the pedal to the floor and hits eighty. The gravel spits out on either side of the road.

The barn, when he reaches it, is in total darkness. He sees the other truck parked at its front.

"Margaret!" he's screaming as he hits the ground running and his heart is banging as he climbs up to the loft.

"Margaret, Margaret!"

It's completely silent.

Then a bat shoots out from under the eaves. It flies out the hayloft window, left standing open. Dust from the hay flies up into his nose.

Above him a rope is still swaying from a beam. But it's empty and has been for all of these months.

"Margaret," he says now, quietly and soft. He sits down on a hay bale and cries.

Maybelleen

Almost Time

In the little adobe jail the sheriff asks her if there is anything she wants. She laughs and turns back to the mirror, donated by a church along with her black crepe dress. The dress is too small and she's ripped it under the right arm.

She tucks in her hair and then pulls it all down. It falls around her shoulders.

"My hair would never stay put," she says to the sheriff.

He nods and turns back to the door.

She looks for a moment out the window to the sky. It's gray and dark though it's getting toward noon.

It's blue. She thinks that and the sheriff says, "It's ten-forty-five. Sure you don't want anything?"

"Thank you, no," she says. And she sits down on her cot. She smooths the rough blanket and feels every fiber.

Suddenly she's unable to catch her breath. It gets stuck and she's frightened, for the first time she's scared.

Throughout the trial she had listened and had even sometimes laughed. She wasn't afraid of the people, wasn't afraid of what they said. A few years earlier they would have had her on a broomstick, consorting with the devil. Since Bill died she'd known there was nothing to do but hang and get it over with and see then what to do.

But now she tastes something black coming up in her throat. Her hands begin shaking and she thinks her heart might stop.

What did it mean.

She'd lived a life dead and dull. Done what she'd been expected to do. Her embroidery was beautiful, couldn't be faulted. She read Latin and some Greek and spoke a fair French. She'd never been pretty, but then she'd never been fat. She always felt a uselessness until she'd met Bill. Was that all she was then, a vacant chest to be filled with another's shining?

But that wasn't right.

She was what she was and Bill had been Bill. Together, they had woken up and shaken the day.

There. That's it.

"You alright, there?" asks the sheriff.

He's miserable about the whole thing. Hanging a woman is monstrous. Why couldn't they have sent her to prison for life? He forgets that he'd called her a murdering bitch during the trial.

"You want some coffee?" he asks, not knowing what he can do.

For a second he's tempted to just let her go.

"No, I'm fine, Sheriff, don't need anything. Do you think it will be alright if I just leave my hair down?"

He nods and turns away.

The sheriff taps his desk and thinks of it all. It is the end of all things, it's crazy is all. After this is over, he's moving away, to a place in the mountains. Somewhere this couldn't happen.

Maybelleen keeps shivering, though she tries her best to hide it. Cold waves run up and down her legs. Will it be quick, she wonders. Will it snap my neck? I don't think I could stand the pain without crying.

The boy's gray, haunted eyes have never left her, the way he'd looked at her, the way he'd seen her. That was love gone wrong, like it had somehow started out straight but taken a wrong turn. Still, after all. After all.

I must think of golden things.

Aaaae aw naw wee, ha na na na.

"And what he told you," says Falls Down in Rain, "is true. It's true."

It is. It is.

She thinks of Bill, filled with holes in her lap. How he'd died and still gone on. Because she believed him. She is the link.

Soon she will find him.

Her hands stop their shaking and she smooths down her hair. "Mama's little baby likes shortnin', shortnin', Mama's little baby likes shortnin' bread."

"You got a pretty voice," says the sheriff.

"Well, it's just something I remembered that I used to sing in time of need. Just a silly song. I wish I believed in angels because I'd sing something else."

"I'll tell you ma'am," says the sheriff, "you been an angel to me. I'll never have a bad word to say."

"Thank you," she says. "Just tell them to remember I died in love. I think that's God, don't you?"

"Reckon so."

The sheriff rises to the pounding at the door.

"I think it's time," he says. His hands are shaking now.

"My word," she says. "Time just goes rushing by, doesn't it. Funny how we never can seem to catch it."

And her legs dissolve and become ether, mere vapor. Her legs are made now of only smoke. But she tries to hide it from the sheriff and by hiding it from him, she tries hard, so hard, to hide it from herself.

For she's walking out the opened door.

Margaret

I sit here again.

All the way over I kept thinking and thinking. Will it be different? Will it matter? Who am I now?

I sit here upon her. It's so dark here and lonely and I can't cry, can't think. I don't know who I am. But after crying so hard, I can't cry anymore—how you feel when you're all cried out and exhausted and open to anything—swollen and given in.

All I hear is dusk sounds. Something rushes up a tree. A squirrel. He sits up there going on and on at me. And if I'm so dead, so dead, why do I feel the cold wet ground clear through my woolen skirt? I wipe my nose and realize that I do. If I'm dead, so dead, why bother.

The grass is cold, still winter brown but just beginning to

smell, to have a scent. And I catch that living fragrance even as I don't want to, I do.

But after a while, after sundown, mostly it's winter quiet, and then an owl begins to call.

The *who who* he is asking is my answer, I find.

Who, I say back. Who indeed?

Because the owl sounds the same as it did when I was little. It's no different and the ground feels exactly the same. And this cold, wet earth registers; feels, all the way down to its veined core.

Does it matter if her blood flows directly right through me? Her idea does and I guess that's what matters in the end.

What is this thing that's always been inside, pounding at me, slapping me, if it wasn't really her?

We can carry nations inside us.

And I am amazed at the calmness around me, at the soft hum of the wind as it grazes the trees.

When I hear him coming, sticks crunching under his anxious boots, I jump up and run to him and bury myself.

"Hello," I say to his tearstained face.

Hello, hello, hello.

This is the time. This is the thing.

Hundreds of faces watched her walking up to the scaffold.

She didn't see them or hear them at all.

The sheriff spoke and the preacher, but it didn't matter. She was deaf to the world and its time.

Before he put the hood on the sheriff said, "Please forgive me. I'm sorry."

"Don't feel that way. I broke the law. Forgive me, too. I only wanted love and I got it."

She looked out on the faces, turned up as though she was performing upon a stage, and at the very edge, she thought she saw a face she knew. His face too, had been turned up, but when he saw her looking, he pulled the brown felt hat far down upon his face.

She smiled out at them, her audience, and held up her head for the dark hood. If only she could have left something that mattered. If only she could have left a living link, not for herself, just for what it had been. That was her failure if there had been one at all.

There was then, still, some proudness, some vanity left no matter how hard she tried to wring it out. That there would be no living link. And dust to dust and then where? The complexity of all the simple things that she, human, knew, howled in her head. From single-celled thing, to this, to her, and some striving ever and ever to leave an imprint and not doing so to feel left at the end, undone.

But she turned back her head, knowing behind the gray clouds the stars still stood and into the stars she leaped.

Then from the silent crowd rang out a single shot. For Maybelleen didn't die an easy death. At the end of the rope she was still alive.

But the bullet found her quick, being aimed, so very carefully, with sure and most sorrowful love.

By the lake I'm sitting where I sit for a spell every day. Through it all I've found, or I've come to know, what it was that the whales always knew as they swam, deep and dark in their circular, oracular world—not from A to B, but in an endless chain that goes 'round and 'round.

And from the bottom of the hill, my daughter comes stumbling on thick baby legs through the bees, who let her pass; unstung. There she is, my girl. My link.

Maybelleen.